KT-132-056

CAVE
OF
SECRETS

MORGAN LLYWELYN is an internationally renowned writer of best-selling historical fiction and contemporary fiction for adults. Her novels for young readers are: *Brian Boru*, *Strongbow* (a Bisto and Reading Association of Ireland award-winner), *The Young Rebels*, *Pirate Queen*, and *Star Dancer*, a contemporary novel about one of her great loves, horses.

CAVE OF SECRETS

MORGAN LLYWELYN

THE O'BRIEN PRESS
DUBLIN

First published 2012 by
The O'Brien Press Ltd,
12 Terenure Road East, Rathgar,
Dublin 6, Ireland.
Tel: +353 1 4923333; Fax: +353 1 4922777
E-mail: books@obrien.ie.
Website: www.obrien.ie
ISBN: 978-1-84717-207-5
Text © copyright Morgan Llywelyn 2012
Copyright for typesetting, layout, editing, design
© The O'Brien Press Ltd

All rights reserved.
No part of this publication may be reproduced
or utilised in any form or by any means,
electronic or mechanical, including photocopying,
recording or in any information storage
and retrieval system, without permission
in writing from the publisher.
British Library Cataloguing-in-Publication Data
A catalogue record for this title is available from the British Library

1 2 3 4 5 6 7 8
12 13 14 15 16

Cover image courtesy of iStockphoto
Printed and bound by CPI Group (UK) Ltd, Croydon, CR0 4YY
The paper used in this book is produced using pulp from managed forests.

The O'Brien Press receives assistance from

DEDICATION

For Maureen, Seamus, and James Langan

ACKNOWLEDGEMENTS

I owe a debt of gratitude to Des Ekin, whose book, *The Stolen Village*, first made me aware of the exciting history of Roaringwater Bay. I am also grateful, as always, to Ide ní Laoghaire for her indispensible editorial skills. No book can be created in a vacuum, and the entire staff at The O'Brien Press has my sincere thanks for their good work on this one.

Contents

PROLOGUE

PROLOGUE

The wind rushes in off the sea like a hag in a billowing cloak. Her streaming hair is made of foam. Her colourless face is a skull. When she shrieks in the night she can freeze the marrow in your bones.

I am not afraid of her. I know she brings treasure.

· · · · · · ·

tom

B oys love caves. A cave is a secret hidden from the rest of the world, smelling of earth and brimming with mystery. Anything might happen in a cave. Something terrible or something wonderful.

On the worst day of his life the boy found a cave.

* * *

Tom tumbled down the face of the cliff, scraping his body against protruding rocks. Shredding his silk stockings. His freckled cheeks were wet with tears. He grasped at random clumps of sea pink but did not really try to stop his fall. Better to break every bone, he thought. Lie smashed to bits at the bottom. Then they would be sorry. If they even noticed. Dying could not be any worse than living.

His feet struck the ground with a thud. He struggled to regain his balance. As the afternoon drew to a close, a cold wind was blowing in from the bay.

Roaringwater Bay.

Leabharlanna Poibli Chathair Baile Átha Cliath

Dublin City Public Libraries

'That evil place deserves its name,' his father often said. Mr Flynn would not allow any of his family to go near the bay. He was determined to keep them safe in a world of their own. 'The bay is infested with savages and barbarians who would as soon kill you as look at you,' Flynn told his son. 'A few years ago a gang of Barbary pirates attacked the fishing village of Baltimore. They kidnapped the English colonists who had settled there and sold all of them – men, women and children – into slavery. Those unfortunate people suffered a fate worse than death. The same thing could happen to you, boy. You could spend the rest of your life in chains in north Africa, with no food in your belly and the lash of the whip on your back every day until you die.'

Mr Flynn's warning had always been enough to keep Tom well away from Roaringwater Bay – until today, when he was more frightened of his father than he was of pirates.

Now he found himself standing on a shingle beach, a coarse mixture of sand and gravel that sloped down towards blue-green water. Huge tumbled boulders and stony out-croppings blocked either end of the beach. Like a pair of sheltering arms, they created a small cove at the foot of the cliff.

The tide was all the way out, but it would return. Looking up the steep face of the cliff, Tom realised he could never climb back. He was trapped. There was no one to help him.

He was alone.

Leabharlanna Poiblí Chathair Baile Átha Cliath
Dublin City Public Libraries

Growing up amid family and servants, he had never thought about what it meant to be alone. With night coming.

Tom's eyes swept frantically around his prison. There was no escape. His heart was hammering so hard he thought it would break his ribs. He struggled not to cry out. If he did, who might come?

Savages. Barbarians.

At last, just above the tide line, he caught sight of what appeared to be a hole in the side of the cliff. It was partially concealed by folds of stony earth. It might be anything, even a shadow. But he ran towards it in desperation.

And found the cave.

The opening was so low he had to creep through on hands and knees like a beaten dog. When he was inside the shadows closed around him. Darkness and silence. *This must be what it's like to be dead.* Drawing his knees against his chest, Tom turned himself into a sad knot of a boy and waited. Waited in misery for whatever awful thing might happen next.

* * *

Everyone called the boy Tom, except his father. William Flynn addressed his son as 'Boy!' – if he spoke to him at all.

With his daughters Flynn was different. Elizabeth, Virginia and Caroline were their father's darlings. He praised them constantly. They fluttered around him like butterflies, competing for his attention. 'Young ladies must practise pleasing men,' he often said. 'That is the way to make a brilliant marriage.'

When he went to Dublin on business, as he did several times a year, he brought back expensive presents for the three girls. Silk ribbons for their hair, Flemish lace for their collars, or satin slippers and cut-glass bottles filled with rose water. On one occasion Elizabeth – his oldest, plainest daughter – was given a silver patch-box filled with tiny stars and moons cut from black velvet. 'Beauty patches are pasted close to eyes or lips to call attention to one's best features,' Flynn explained. 'All the great beauties are using them now.'

After his most recent journey to Dublin, Flynn gave Tom a hobby-horse. It was far too childish for a thirteen-year-old boy. The body was nothing but an ordinary broom handle. The head had been roughly hacked from a block of wood. The eyes were painted on. One eye stared upwards; the other looked sideways.

'I bought it for you in the capital,' Flynn said. 'A man was selling them on a street corner.'

Tom was dismayed. Did his father think he was still a baby? He accepted the hobby-horse with a muttered 'Thank you,' and propped it behind the chest in the corner of his bedchamber, as far out of sight as possible.

For his wife the man had a much nicer gift. He proudly presented Catherine Flynn with a highly polished rosewood

14

box, bound in brass and fastened by a padlock. He made a ceremony of giving her the key. She turned it in the lock and lifted the lid, then looked up in surprise. When she spoke her voice was as soft as a whisper, too soft even for a recognisable accent. Her family were used to straining to hear her words. 'I fear you have been swindled, William,' she murmured.

'What do you mean?'

'There is nothing in this chest but dry leaves.'

Flynn barked a laugh. 'Me? Swindled? You should know better than that, Kate. Every step I take is carefully planned. Those dry leaves, as you call them, are valuable. They must be kept under lock and key. Steeping just a few in boiling water produces a most refreshing beverage. In Dublin they call it China ale, or China tea, and predict it may someday replace coffee. The English East India Company has begun bringing tea from the east on their clipper ships. They hope to create a market for it as far afield as the colony of Virginia in the New World. And I hope to buy shares in the East India Company,' he added smugly.

Mrs Flynn raised her eyebrows, which were as black and as delicate as a butterfly's antennae. 'Shares?'

'Do not bother your head, m'dear, women cannot possibly understand such things,' Flynn assured her. 'All you need to know is that East India shares are an excellent investment. They are closely held, but I have a talent for making important friends. To such a man anything is possible, eh? Now lock that tea chest. Keep the key on your girdle with the other household keys, and never entrust it to a servant. You know these locals would steal us blind if we let them.'

'I know, dear,' she said. Softly.

* * *

The worst day of Tom's life had begun pleasantly enough. A warm day in early June, with only a few shreds of ragged cloud in the west. As was their custom, the family had gathered in their private oratory for morning prayer, led by Elizabeth. Mr Flynn rarely visited the tiny chapel – except when he paid a priest to say Mass – but he did put in an appearance at breakfast later. He gobbled down his food and left the table before anyone else had finished.

After breakfast Mrs Flynn had returned to her bed-chamber, where she spent much of her time. Tom's mother was a thin, pale woman who grew thinner and paler each year. Elizabeth went to her own chamber, while her younger sisters began trying on their party frocks. Satin bodices tightly laced, taffeta skirts lined with sarsenet. They trotted from one room to another to admire themselves in every looking-glass. A maid was kept busy rearranging their hair.

A gala event was planned for Roaringwater House that evening. William Flynn had often entertained the gentry of West Cork, but never before on such a lavish scale. The event was to announce the betrothal of his eldest daughter. At age twenty-three, Elizabeth Flynn had been considered a spinster until her father arranged a match for her. The prospective bridegroom was one of his business associates.

Herbert Fox, the son of an English seaman, owned his own shipping business in Cobh. He was twice widowed and three times Elizabeth's age. But as Flynn had explained to his wife, 'The influence of landed Catholics like ourselves is fading fast, Kate. We need Protestant friends like Herbert Fox. He is a shrewd businessman and a good catch for our daughter.'

'Surely we could do better for her, William. Mr Fox is so ... coarse.'

Her husband sought to reassure her. 'Herbert speaks the language of the docks, which is not surprising. But I shall find husbands of more quality for the other girls. It is just a matter of moving in the right circles.'

* * *

The servants had been preparing the house for weeks. The rushes had been swept from the floor of the room Mr Flynn called 'the great hall', which ran the width of the house. The bare stones had been scoured with sand. A Persian rug with a design of peacocks and horses now lay in the exact centre of the hall, where it glowed like a West Cork sunset.

17

Tapestries picturing court scenes and hunting scenes hung on the walls. The chairs and benches were fitted with cushions embroidered in silk by the ladies of the family. A dark, heavily carved chest in the newly fashionable Jacobean style was prominently displayed.

No effort was spared to provide entertainment for the expected guests. Men and women alike loved to gamble, so special tables had been fitted out for Backgammon and Dice and Five Card. A constant supply of refreshments was on hand. As soon as the guests arrived ruby port would be served to the men, and sweet sherry offered to the women. Musicians were travelling by coach from Bantry to provide music.

A level area beyond the house was roped off for wrestling matches. The ground was raked clean of stones and rolled to make it firm. Armloads of spiky furze were stuffed into tubs and set at each corner of the arena, where their golden blooms blazed like fires. Fresh limewash was applied to the stones bordering the carriage drive, and a new gravel path was laid to the front door of the house.

'Richard Boyle, the Earl of Cork, is the special guest,' William Flynn stressed to his servants. 'He is the most important man in Munster, maybe in the whole of Ireland. When the earl arrives he must be favourably impressed. My property must bloom for him on the day, even if it wilts on the morrow.'

Early on the morning of the party, mouth-watering aromas

began to waft from the kitchen in the basement. In honour of the occasion a special dinner was being prepared. There would be heaping platters of roasted marrow bones, apple-fed pork and stubble-fed goose, game pies and ox tongue and creamed kidneys, boiled beef seasoned with applesauce and horseradish, carrots and cabbages awash with butter. The menu included thrushes baked in pastry nests and roast swan fitted back into its own skin. Cook had outdone herself. To the dismay of the scullery maid, every pan and pot in the house was dirty by noon.

While everyone else was busy, Tom Flynn wandered about the house with his hands in his pockets, idly watching the final preparations. He was wearing a fitted coat of dark blue broadcloth, a white cambric shirt with lace on the cuffs, a snug waistcoat with brass buttons, and a pair of fawn-coloured knee breeches buttoned over white silk stockings. Landowners' children past the age of infancy were always dressed in miniature versions of their parents' clothes.

Tom's clothes looked adult, but he was not treated as an adult. Everyone knew his mother still thought of him as her little boy. Her baby.

Late in the afternoon he found his eldest sister huddled at the top of the front staircase. She had been crying. A clumsily applied beauty patch only called attention to her swollen eyes.

Tom sat down beside her. 'What's the matter, Lizzie? Why

aren't you getting ready for your party?'

She broke into fresh sobs.

Tom was alarmed. He put an awkward arm around her shoulders. He had little in common with his sisters and had never tried to hug one before.

Elizabeth angrily shrugged off his embrace. 'Let go of me.'

Tom's arm drew back like a snail retreating into its shell. 'But you're in tears and I want to help.'

'I am not in tears,' she insisted. 'I never weep. I'm the happiest girl in the world. Sixteen months from now I'll be a married woman. Isn't that wonderful?' She interrupted herself with a violent hiccup. After a few embarrassed moments she said in a loud voice, 'Just go away, Tom, and leave me alone!'

'Boy!' William Flynn shouted from elsewhere in the house. 'If you're upsetting your sister on this day of all days, I'll stripe your legs with leather until they bleed!'

From her room, Tom's mother called out anxiously, 'What's wrong? Is there trouble?' The boy knew it would not help to get her involved. Catherine Flynn never stood up to her husband.

Before she could appear, Tom dashed down the stairs – only to find his father waiting for him at the bottom. 'I curse the hour you were born, boy! This time I am going to kill you, begog I will!' Flynn swung a massive fist at his son's head.

Ducking the blow, Tom fled from Roaringwater House. And found his cave. Now he was wrapped in its smothering darkness. Like being buried alive.

Tom forced himself to get to his feet. He felt less helpless standing upright. He could sense the ceiling of the cave just above his head. But when he reached out, his hands touched empty space. His nose wrinkled at the musty odour of bat droppings. 'Whew!' he said in disgust.

At the rear of the cave, something laughed.

• • • • • • •

CHAPTER TWO

DONAL

tom's scalp prickled with alarm. 'Who's there?'

The laughter stopped.

As Tom's eyes adjusted to the gloom he saw a shape emerge from the shadows. A boyish voice with a lilting accent inquired, 'And who is it that's asking?'

'I am called Tom Flynn. Who are you? Are you Irish?'

'Are ye not Irish yourself, with a name like that?' the stranger challenged. 'Were you born in Ireland?'

'I was.'

'And your father's fathers? Were they born in Ireland too?'

'They were.'

'Then why talk in a foreign language?'

Tom was puzzled. 'Do you mean English? But we speak English at home.'

'We speak English at home,' the other boy mimicked. 'And where is your home? London, is it?'

'I live at Roaringwater House. My father built it before I was born.'

'Only the *Sasanach* give names to their houses.' There was contempt in the boy's voice.

The fright Tom had felt turned to anger. 'I'm not telling you any more until I know who you are.'

The stranger laughed again, the merry laugh of someone with not a care in the world. '*Is mise Donal*,' he replied.

'You are called Donal?'

'So you do understand Irish.'

'Only a few words. Our servants speak Irish among themselves,' said Tom.

'Servants!' The other boy sounded scornful. 'And what do servants do that ye can't do for yourself?'

Tom could not think of an answer.

Donal came a step closer. 'You don't belong here.'

'I don't belong anywhere,' Tom said ruefully. He was surprised to be admitting his feelings to a stranger.

Donal took another step forward. Tom could smell him now. Sweat and smoke and salt sea wind, and something else. A wild smell. '*I* belong here,' Donal boasted. Flinging his arms wide, he filled the empty space with himself. 'I'm the guard!'

'Why would anyone guard an empty cave?'

Donal said slyly, 'You'd like to know that, would you?' He caught the other boy by the arm. 'Let's go outside, Tom Flynn. There's nothing to see in here.'

* * *

William Flynn stood with his feet planted wide and his fists on his hips. When he lowered his head, the stocky man looked like a bull about to charge. 'Where is that wretched boy, eh?' he demanded of his wife. 'Is he deliberately trying to ruin things for me?'

'Of course not,' she said, keeping her eyes lowered so she did not see the anger in his face.

'Are you certain, Kate? Do you know what just happened? For an hour I had been doing my best to win Richard Boyle's confidence. I said I was trying, in my modest way, to create a gentleman's country estate here like the magnificent place he built for himself near Lismore.

'I was trying to work the conversation around to my other ambitions, when the earl commented that more Protestants are entering the Irish parliament. The balance of power is tilting their way, he said, so the time is right to extend the plantation of Munster. That means taking more land away from Catholic landowners and giving it to loyal Protestants.'

Flynn waited for his wife to react. She waited for him to reveal why this was upsetting him.

After a moment he continued. 'Parliament, with Boyle as its most powerful member, oversees the plantation scheme. Some friends of his are eager to acquire plantation lands in this area as a speculative venture. Through a deal with the earl, they will receive the properties free of charge and then sell them on at inflated prices, making a huge profit for everyone involved. Except the original landowner, of course.

'When the earl told me about this, I regretted having made such an effort to impress him with my property. As a Catholic landowner, I must find a way to keep it from being seized. Thinking fast, I suggested that a local landowner like myself would be perfect for organising the scheme. All I would require was a central base to act from. Boyle is a clever man, he knew at once that I was hinting at a position with the Dublin administration.'

'You are a clever man too, William,' his wife murmured.

But her praise did not cheer him. Instead he scowled. 'Unfortunately, at that very moment a servant rushed in claiming that Thomas had run away. Richard Boyle heard it all. He was standing right there with his son Roger, Baron Broghill. How could the earl respect a man who cannot govern his own child? You should have seen the expression on his face. Thanks to that miserable son of yours, now the earl would not trust me to mind mice at a crossroads.'

She laid a gentle hand on her husband's arm. 'Tom is your son too, William. And I am sure the earl will not hold such a small incident against you. If he has sons he must know something of boys. Besides, Tom would never run away. He is merely playing one of his pranks.'

'So much the worse for him if he is!' Flynn sprayed spittle

in his anger. 'I'll cane him within an inch of his life!'

His wife took half a step back to avoid the shower. 'Your guests are waiting,' she reminded him. 'Surely you can mend your fences with the earl. As you said yourself, you have a gift for making people like you. Flatter him and tell him some of your best stories. Meanwhile, perhaps I might lie down for a while?' She looked at him hopefully, seeking his permission.

* * *

Outside the cave the light was fading. Tom saw that his arm was being tightly gripped by a boy smaller than he, though obviously stronger. Donal's skin was chapped by wind and weather. His shaggy black hair fell to his shoulders. His eyes were a brilliant blue. Salt-stained woollen trews, with a bit of rope for a belt, were his only garment. His upper body was as bare as his feet.

Donal was not impressed by Tom's greater size. His fingers already had discovered that the newcomer's arm lacked muscle. His cheeks were as plump as a baby's. Although Tom's clothes were torn from his scramble down the cliff, his brown hair remained tied at the nape of his neck with a stiff grosgrain ribbon. There were silver buckles on his leather shoes.

Donal knew he could take those silver buckles if he wanted. 'Your clothes would make a cat laugh,' he said.

Tom was insulted. 'This is what men wear!'

'Not here, they don't. It would get in the way.'

'In the way of what?'

Donal narrowed his eyes. 'You ask too many questions.'

'I don't ask as many as you,' Tom snapped.

The two boys glared at each other. For a moment they were close to blows. Then the moment passed, and they laughed instead.

Donal released Tom's arm. 'You made enough noise coming down that cliff for a whole company of soldiers,' he said in a friendlier tone. 'What was chasing you? Wolves?'

Tom resisted the urge to rub his arm. 'Something worse,' he replied ruefully. 'I was running from my father. He said he would kill me.'

Donal grinned, revealing a missing tooth. 'Not a day passes but my father threatens to roast me over a slow fire. He doesn't mean it.'

'Mine does,' said Tom. 'He hates me.'

'You must have got it wrong. Men value their sons above everything. My father and I are as close as the fingers on your hand. He is *An Rí* – the king,' Donal added proudly, translating to be sure the other boy understood.

'Now you have it wrong. Charles Stuart is the king.'

'Phah!' Donal said. 'He's only the king of the *Sasanach*. My father, Muiris, is a chieftain. A *real* king.'

Tom was not sure what Donal meant. The education of

CAVE OF SECRETS

William Flynn's children did not include the Irish culture. 'You know where I live,' he said to Donal, 'so tell me where you live.'

Donal turned and pointed in the dusk. 'My people live a short distance down the coast, you can't see the place from here. They were fishermen for generations.'

'What do you mean, "were"? Don't they fish now?'

The other boy hesitated. 'We still make our living from the sea,' he said.

'Do you have a large family?'

'There was a large family. Now there's only Maura and me.' Donal's merry face had turned to stone. His eyes warned Tom not to ask more questions.

But curiosity was too strong. 'What happened to them? Were they taken ill?'

Donal stared bleakly into space. 'Before I was born, my parents had three other boys and another girl. They died of fever. People say it comes on the ships sometimes.'

Tom wished he could take back his words. He fumbled for something to say which would not cause pain to the other boy. 'I don't have any brothers either,' he offered.

Donal's expression softened. 'Maura's almost as good as a brother, even if she is a girl. She's only little but she's as cute as a pet fox.'

'She doesn't sound much like my sisters. I have three without a thought in their heads. As useless as a platter of

28

air, the lot of them.'

'How do you know? Do you ever talk to them?'

Tom looked startled. 'Talk? To girls?'

'Maura and I talk all the time.'

'How old is she?'

'Younger than me. Four summers.'

'How old are you, Donal?'

'Almost eleven summers. And yourself?'

'A bit older than that,' Tom replied, embarrassed to admit his exact age to the smaller but stronger boy.

From the corner of his eye Donal glimpsed a flash of light in the bay. He stiffened in concentration. The light flashed again. Twice. 'You can't stay here, Tom Flynn,' he said briskly. 'You have to go back where you came from.'

'I can't! I mean … I can't climb that cliff.'

'Is that all? There are easier ways. Follow me; you'll be home before hounds can scratch fleas.' Seizing Tom's arm again, Donal ran up the beach.

The wind howled over Roaringwater Bay.

CHAPTER THREE

IN THE MIST

t om was crawling into bed when he heard footsteps in the passage outside his door. He pulled the bedclothes over his head and lay still.

While he was with Donal some of the other boy's confidence had rubbed off on him. For a brief time he could imagine that he too was part of a close family, and had a father who would be glad to see him again. That confidence was gone now.

A woman carrying a candle in a pewter candlestick entered the bed-chamber. She was shaking her head and muttering to herself. Her collapsed mouth was toothless, her shoulders stooped with age. A few locks of grey hair clung to a pink scalp. Eithne had been nurse to all four of the Flynn children. Now she was demoted to housemaid. She did not know what would become of her when she was too old and crippled for even that work. William Flynn was not a charitable man.

Her eyes swept the room. The walls were covered with

horsehair plaster. A chest with drawers stood in one corner. The floor was bare. The only window was secured at night by heavy timber shutters. Below the window was a small cabinet with space underneath for a chamber pot.

The panel giving access to the bed-closet was firmly closed.

The ancient oak forests that once carpeted Ireland were nearly gone. Cut down to build England's warships. Burned for charcoal so Irish chieftains would have no place to hide. The enclosed bed that sheltered Tom from drafts was made of deal painted to look like oak. His father had warned him not to scratch the finish. 'I paid the king's coin for that piece. Damage it and you will sleep on the floor.'

In a bed-closet which pretended to be Irish oak, Tom tried to pretend he was back in the cave.

He felt a tickle in his nose. Try as he might, he could not hold back a mighty sneeze.

Eithne scurried to the bed-closet and slid back the panel. With one gnarled finger she poked at a mountain range of rumpled blankets. 'Master Tom? Is it yourself under there?'

Reluctantly, the boy sat up, yawning and stretching as if he had been fast asleep.

'We're worn to the bone searching for you,' the old woman complained. 'When you didn't come for your supper I thought for sure you'd scarpered. It fair put the heart cross-wise in me.'

At the mention of food Tom's stomach rumbled. 'What was my supper?'

'Barley soup and suet pudding. I would not let them give you any of that rich party food. Och, you were wicked to disappear, lad. I was blamed, even if you're not my babby any more.'

'What happened wasn't your fault. It was just ...' Tom paused, knowing he did not have to explain to her. Eithne knew how harshly William treated his only son. 'I thought it best to stay out of his sight for a while, so I went as far away as I could. After dark I returned and sneaked up the back stairs. I've been in my bed ever since.'

That much was true. But he had left out the bit in the middle. The bit where he found the cave. And made a friend.

When they had parted at the top of the cliff, Donal had said, 'Now you know the way, Tom Flynn, come back again if you like.'

'Tomorrow?'

Donal shook his head. 'Not tomorrow. Give it ...' He counted out the fingers on his lean hand. 'Give it three days.'

'Will you be here then?'

'I might,' said Donal with a shrug. 'Will you come?'

'I might,' Tom replied. And shrugged.

The two boys laughed.

'Take care that no one follows you,' Donal warned as they parted. 'Come down through that cut in the cliff face the way I showed you, and give a whistle at the mouth of the cave. Like this, listen.'

Tom had listened carefully.

* * *

Eithne went to tell Tom's mother that he was home and safe, then brought the boy some bread and cheese. While he gobbled the meal she sat beside him. As he wiped the last crumbs from his mouth he said, 'Sing me a lullaby, Eithne.'

The old woman smiled. 'It's a long time since I sang *suantraí* to one of the childer.'

'You know the one I like best. Please?' The gentry were not supposed to say please to servants, but Tom said it anyway – as long as he was out of his father's hearing. He snuggled down into the bed and pulled the quilt up to his chin, waiting.

Eithne heaved a sigh and settled herself on a three-legged stool beside the bed. Her cracked voice filled the chamber. '*Come and take a ride with me upon my magic pony*,' she sang lovingly. '*Fast and far we'll travel all the live long day.*'

Tom fell asleep before she finished the song. He awoke to find himself alone. Eithne had opened the shutters over his window before she left, and his bed-chamber was rosy with dawn light. He expected his father to come bursting in at any moment to punish him. When he did not, the boy hurriedly dressed and left the room.

The doors leading to the other chambers on the landing were firmly closed. Behind them lay deep pools of silence.

Tom made his way to the front staircase. He tiptoed down with one hand on the railing.

The great hall of Roaringwater House resembled a battle-field. The new Persian rug had been slashed by a sword. The front panel of the Jacobean chest was bashed in. Chairs and benches were overturned and broken. Cushions were ripped open and sodden with wine. Candles had guttered in their sconces; the wax ran down the walls. Men whom William Flynn called the most important in the land lay sprawled drunkenly on the floor. One wore a soup tureen on his head like a helmet.

They smell worse than a cave of bats, Tom thought to himself.

He did not see his father amongst the fallen, but he did not look too closely. Still on tiptoe, he left the house. No one stirred. The heavy door creaked on its iron hinges as it closed behind him. The early morning air was sweet and clean.

Although Roaringwater House was built of rubblestone, the three-storey central block had a limestone façade. Low wings extended on either side. One wing contained the stables, the other was occupied by the servants – with the exception of three who had small rooms at the top of the house; they were the cook, the housekeeper, and Simon, the steward, who performed a number of tasks.

The mullioned windows at the front of the house were fitted with specially cut glass panes. There were no large windows at the rear. No sweeping view of the spectacular coastline with its rugged headlands, its numerous islands set like jewels in the gleaming water. Roaringwater House turned its back on the bay. William Flynn's gaunt grey residence faced northeast towards distant Dublin. The seat of power.

The tenants on William Flynn's land worked as servants to pay rent for their smallholdings, which were nowhere near his house. Tom and his sisters lived in a cocoon of their father's making. They never met the servants' children, who received no education and were not considered fit playmates. Beneath the broad and windswept sky there was no boy of Tom's age. He had no companion and nothing to do except for the games he invented for himself. His favourite had always been to pretend he was a general leading his imaginary troops to one victory after another – each the result of his clever strategy. He still played the game, even if he was getting a bit old for it.

In the autumn a tutor would ride out from Bantry to spend four days a week at Roaringwater House. Flynn had not sent any of his children away to school. 'There are too many disturbing influences in Ireland now,' he explained. The girls' education had long since concluded, but this year Tom would be instructed in classical history, algebra, gentlemanly deportment and Italian art. Autumn seemed far away.

35

With no particular destination in mind, Tom wandered about 'The Park' as his father called the barren landscape surrounding the house. Stony land with shallow soil where only furze and heather thrived. The roses his mother planted in front of the house every year died the following year. Along the deeply rutted drive with its gleaming white borders several empty carriages waited. From the stables came the sound of an impatient hoof pawing on cobbles.

Otherwise there were no signs of life.

Tom ambled along until he came to a large patch of torn-up turf, the site of yesterday's wrestling matches.

Wrestling was one of the most popular sports in Ireland. Peasant and gentry alike competed, though not against one another. A lot of betting went on. Each wrestler wore a wide leather belt around his body. He would seize his opponent's belt with one hand and wait for the signal. When it came, the two struggled until one broke the other's grip in any way he could, and then threw him down with all the strength he had. There were no other rules.

Donal would be good at wrestling, Tom said to himself.

Three days. Why wait three days? Why not go to the cave now and see if Donal was there?

Glancing towards the house to be sure no one saw him, the boy set off at a brisk walk. Savages and barbarians, he thought to himself. Barbary pirates. What nonsense. Those are just threats my father makes to keep me on a chain, like the mastiff who guards the stables. I'm not a dog. Or a servant. I don't have to take orders. I'll wager Donal doesn't take orders.

The more distance Tom put between himself and the house, the better he felt. At first he did not notice that a sea mist was blowing in from the bay. It rolled in shifting swirls, gradually obscuring the landscape. When Tom realised he was surrounded by a thick white cloud he stopped walking.

The mist was eerie. Magical. Sound was muffled. The boy's skin felt cold and damp. His lips and eyelashes were wet. Tiny droplets on his clothing like little pearls. He considered turning around and going home. Instead he whistled a cheerful tune and resumed walking. Walking in the clouds through a magical world of his own.

When he was sure he must be near the cliffs, he heard voices on the wind. The voices became clearer, became men shouting. Tom held his breath to listen but the voices stopped. It must have been a trick of the wind. He walked on. Then he heard another shout.

A blaze of golden furze shone through the mist in front of him. He recognised that furze. It clung to the edge of the cliff above the cave. He carefully parted its spiky branches and peered down. He could not see the beach for the mist. Yet he had the distinct feeling that someone was there.

Tom thought it best to keep out of sight until he knew what was happening. He sat down crosslegged behind the screen of the furze and listened with all his might. To the muted roar of the wind. To the delicate whisper of the mist.

His imagination went galloping off without him. Had Donal been warning him when he said not to come back for three days? Was the danger real? Yet Donal had not seemed afraid. But Donal was not down there, either.

Or if he was, he was in the cave. He could be tied up in there, the prisoner of pirates!

Roaring at the top of his lungs, courageous General Thomas Flynn plunged over the edge of the cliff to rescue his new friend.

CHAPTER FOUR

MAURA

Caroline Flynn threaded a blue satin ribbon through her dark ringlets, the corkscrew ringlets she painstakingly rolled up on strips of rag every night. She was very proud of her hair. She studied her reflection in the looking glass. 'I should be the bride,' she said. 'I'm 'way prettier than Lizzie. I'm the only one of us who looks like Mother.'

'You're the youngest,' Virginia reminded her, 'so you can't marry until after I do. And I cannot marry until Lizzie is wed. Be happy for her.'

'How can I? Have you seen the face on him? That old man looks like a wadded-up handkerchief full of–'

'Don't, Caro!' Virginia cried. But she was laughing.

'Would you want to marry him?' her younger sister asked.

Virginia's laugh faded. 'I suppose I shall have to marry someone, but I hope Father finds a more handsome man for me. If I had my choice, Caro – and promise you won't breathe a word of this to Mother – I would rather not be married at all.'

Caroline was astonished. 'Not married? But what would you do, Ginny?'

'Paint,' her sister replied firmly. 'Landscapes, I think, or maybe even portraits. Painting is the one thing I do really well and I love it. Mr Beasley said my watercolours were very nice.'

'He had to say so, he was our tutor and Father was paying him. Besides, you can't spend your life painting.'

'Some people do,' said Virginia. 'Mr Beasley told me that Irish artists have even gone abroad to study. Imagine living in Paris!' Her eyes were shining.

Caroline shook her head until her ringlets bounced. 'Father would never let you do that, Ginny. He'll find a suitable Catholic husband for you, perhaps one of the Old English whose ancestors came to Ireland with Strongbow. Then you will be the mistress of a house like this one and have lots of beautiful clothes to wear.'

'Sugar and cream!' Virginia burst out – the only 'bad language' her mother allowed. 'I do not intend to spend my life buried in the country. Thank goodness we may be moving to Dublin.'

Caroline gasped. 'Dublin? Do you mean it? When? We'll need new frocks and bonnets and we must learn the new dances and–'

'You silly goose,' Virginia interrupted, 'there is more to life than clothes and dances. Father is hoping for a political

40

appointment in the capital.'

Her sister stared at her. 'Who told you so?'

'No one told me. I keep my mouth closed and my ears open. That's how I learn things. Before the party I heard him tell Mother that the pieces were falling into place.'

* * *

Falling down the cliff, Tom realised he had made a stupid mistake. He was only a boy, how could he possibly face down a gang of kidnappers and rescue his friend? They would take him too. He would be beaten and tied up and ...

He hit the beach with a thud that knocked the breath out of him. Screwing his eyes tightly shut, he waited for the next awful thing to happen to him.

Nothing happened. All he heard was the sound of the waves and the patter of a few stones, displaced by his fall, as they struck the ground around him. He opened his eyes. He saw no pirates, no captives, no other living being.

When he stood up he noticed a wide gouge in the sand. It began at the mouth of the cave. He approached the cave warily and peered inside, but saw nothing. Only shadows. He tried Donal's whistle, then listened to its eerie echo die away without an answer.

He turned and followed the strange track to the water's edge, where it disappeared.

Tom shaded his eyes with his hand and looked out across the bay. The sky was spread with clouds as thick as clotted cream. Ropes of foam were dragging the waves across the water. Two small boats with sails raised were speeding towards the nearest island. Already they were too far away for him to make out any details. A captive could be lying, bound hand and foot, in the bottom of one of them.

And there was nothing Tom could do about it.

He watched until the boats rounded the island and disappeared from his view. Then he trudged home with a heavy heart. His mood lifted when Virginia said his father had just departed unexpectedly for Dublin. Flynn had not mentioned Tom at all before leaving. The recent incident between them seemed to be forgotten.

* * *

The boy waited for two more days before returning to the bay. He followed the narrow downward path Donal had shown him, zigzagging between sharp rocks. On the beach everything looked as before, except that the channel leading to the sea had disappeared. Swept away by the tide.

When he spied a piece of driftwood on the sand, Tom picked it up and brandished it like a sword. 'I'll save you, Donal!' he cried, pretending he was a man, with a man's power: Thomas Flynn, brave general of His Majesty's forces–

'I don't need saving,' a voice called.

Tom turned around. Donal was clambering with ease over the nearest spur of rocks. 'I'm glad you remembered about the three days,' he said.

Tom did not contradict him. 'You can trust me.'

'My father says trust must be earned.'

'Your father the king?'

'My father the king,' Donal repeated solemnly. 'What were you doing just now?'

'Pretending to be a general. Don't you ever play that game?'

'I don't play games,' said Donal. 'I work. Today I'm harvesting the shore.'

'I thought your work was guarding the cave,' Tom teased.

'That's part of it. So is gathering seaweed, and collecting firewood, and catching fish, and mending nets, and helping repair boats, and—'

Tom stared at him. 'You really do work.'

'We work all the time.'

'We?'

Donal put two fingers in his mouth and gave a piercing whistle, quite unlike the one Tom had practised. Within moments a tiny girl came scrambling over the stony barrier at the other end of the beach. The mass of tumbled boulders seemed no obstacle to her.

She wore a simple, homespun gown. A flannel petticoat

peeped from beneath the hem of her skirt. Tied around her waist was a blue apron the colour of her eyes. She had made a sling for carrying driftwood by holding up the corners of her apron. Seeing the stranger, she dropped the wood with a clatter. 'Who's that, Don-don?'

'Tom Flynn,' Donal said. 'He's all right, he's my friend.'

The little face peeping through tangled curls broke into a smile. 'Tomflynn,' the child said, running the name together to make a single word. 'Hello, Tomflynn.' She bent to gather up the spilt wood.

Tom crouched down to help her. She pushed him away with a grubby little hand. 'Don't need help,' she cheerfully asserted.

Tom looked up at Donal. 'I suppose this is Maura?'

'She is Maura. Isn't she a clinker? There's no finer *cailín* on this side of the bay.'

The little girl fixed bright blue eyes on Tom's face. 'Mine,' she declared, reaching out to grab the piece of driftwood in his hand. In the next breath she said, 'Are you a prostint?'

'A what?'

'She means a Protestant,' her brother explained.

'I'm a Catholic,' said Tom. 'Does it matter?'

'Not to us,' Donal told him.

Tom spent a morning like none in his memory. Maura insisted on looking for 'pretty' seashells. Tom's first discovery was a glossy, cone-shaped shell vividly striped with orange.

Even Donal was impressed. 'I've never seen one like that before. Have you?'

'I've never seen any seashells,' Tom admitted.

The other two looked at him open-mouthed. He did not know whether to be proud or embarrassed.

They gathered more driftwood from the beach and showed Tom how to harvest seaweed. The driftwood was for fuel, Donal explained, and the seaweed would go into the cooking pot.

'I didn't know you could eat it,' said Tom.

'You have to know which ones,' the other boy told him. 'Some are good for eating and others are good for healing.'

'What else do you eat?'

'Ev'ry fish there is,' Maura piped up.

Donal laughed. 'Not quite,' he said. 'You wouldn't eat a jellyfish even if you were starving to death. But mackerel, *áthasach*! Great food. We eat mackerel from summer's end until Christmas. We eat herring too, and cod and pilchard and seal meat, and badger when we can get one, and birds' eggs and every kind of shellfish ...' he interrupted himself to point to a jet of water spurting from a hole in the sand, '... like that one. There's a razor clam.' He pounced as swiftly as a cat, and stood up holding a long, tightly closed shell.

That day Tom received a thorough instruction in the varieties of shellfish which made the bay their home. Mussels and limpets and cockles and winkles, shrimp and crabs and even sea urchins, which were terrifying to look at but "lishus!" according to Maura. Tom had thought of Roaringwater Bay as nothing more than a vast sheet of water. Now he realised it was an immense larder, filled with items more interesting than suet pudding.

Again and again his eyes returned to the gleaming expanse of the bay. The dancing waves, the shifting clouds. The constant interplay of birds in the air and along the shore. Kittiwakes and blackbacks, terns and shags and cormorants. Larks soaring high in the air, their song falling to earth like liquid sunshine.

Tom said, 'I never knew the bay was so beautiful.'

'Beautiful?' Donal was surprised. He had never thought of the bay as beautiful though he saw it almost every day of his life. 'Can't you see it from your house?' he asked Tom.

'Only in the distance.'

'Does that make a difference?'

Tom nodded. 'All the difference in the world. Do those islands out there have names?'

'They do have names,' said Donal. 'Every place made by God has a name. The big island at the mouth of the bay is Dún na Séad, the Fortress of the Jewels. You might have heard it called by its English name, Cape Clear. When all the land belonged to the Gael, Dún na Séad was a kingdom with its own king.'

'A king like your father?'

'He had a larger territory than my father does,' the other

boy said. 'Look where I'm pointing now: there are the three
Calf Islands, and there is Long Island, and Coney, and Castle
– which has a castle on it – and there are the Skeams, and
yonder is the Horse, and the Hare, and–'

'Do people live on the islands?'

'On most of them. Farming is hard, but they have the sea
to feed them.'

'Are the islanders savages?'

Donal glared at Tom. 'They're no different from Maura
and me.'

'I didn't mean–'

'Only the *Sasanach* would ask a question like that,' Donal
went on angrily.

Tom's own temper surfaced. 'I'm not a foreigner!'

'*Sasanach* doesn't mean foreigner. It means Saxon. Eng-
lishman, Protestant, *Saxon*.' Donal spat out the word as if it
tasted bad.

Tom retorted, 'I'm not a Saxon, either!'

Donal held his eyes a moment longer, then looked down.
'I know it,' he said.

Before saying goodbye that day, Tom offered Donal the
orange-striped shell.

'I can't take that,' Donal protested. 'You found it, it's yours.'

'I want you to have it,' Tom insisted. 'It's an apology.'

Afterwards Tom Flynn would recall the summer of 1639 as
the best time of his life.

CHAPTER FIVE

THE SWIMMER

N ow that the formal announcement had been made, preparations for Elizabeth Flynn's wedding began in earnest. The ceremony was scheduled for the following year. In the meantime there was much to be done. The bride's mother was expected to make all the necessary social arrangements. She must also prepare Roaringwater House for a much grander occasion than a mere engagement party. Mr Flynn wanted numerous repairs and improvements made to the house. The servants must be prodded into exceptional activity.

Tom's mother had no talent for prodding servants. She could not even raise her voice to them. She simply made suggestions – and usually forgot to follow up.

In the end, Virginia undertook the organising. She made countless lists for herself on bits of paper. Any drawer in the house might be opened only to find one of Virginia's 'To Do' lists inside. She had earnest conversations with Simon about clearing drains, and demanded that Cook create new pastries.

She bullied the housemaids, even old Eithne, and occasionally tried to give orders to Missus, the housekeeper. Caroline teased her, but she took her self-imposed task seriously.

Elizabeth Flynn sought to avoid it all. She often went to her bed-chamber and closed the door. Her mother had taught by example that when a lady's door was closed, she must not be disturbed. She was in her sanctuary, a place where she could pray and think and dream.

The windows of Elizabeth's sanctuary were draped with damask. The sheets were bleached linen. A gilt-framed oil painting of King Charles stared down from one wall. There were portraits of the king throughout Roaringwater House. Some were clumsy paintings by amateurs, like the one in Elizabeth's room. Two or three were good miniatures in silver and gold frames. These were prominently placed where any visitor would see them.

Charles Stuart, son of James VI, grandson of Mary, Queen of Scots, and King of Great Britain and Ireland, was a slightly built man. He had a Scottish accent and a stammer that his portraits did not reveal.

In her sanctuary Elizabeth often sat in a window embrasure like a princess in a tower, watching for a prince to come riding to her rescue. Her prince never came. But one morning she did notice her brother riding away from Roaringwater House. Tom was cantering along on the rubbishy stick horse their father had given him. And he was singing. The words drifted back to the watcher in the window. '*Come and take a ride with me upon my magic pony ...*'

Dreams and fancies, Elizabeth thought bitterly. No good can come of that.

As far back as she could remember, her father had chased one dream after another. Very few of them came true. Only Roaringwater House. And soon, this awful marriage. Elizabeth envied Tom. Boys had it all, they could do anything they liked. No one cared about women's dreams.

'I'm being traded like a carriage horse, and I hate it,' Elizabeth complained to Virginia later that day.

'Don't be ridiculous, Lizzie. What's so bad about marrying a man who has money? If I had money I could go to Paris to paint and no one would stop me. Everyone needs money, even the king. He imposes more and more taxes because he has to pay the debts left from his wars with France and Spain. And the uprising in Scotland is costing him another fortune.'

'How do you know about all that, Ginny?'

Her sister was exasperated. 'Sugar and cream! Am I the only person in this house who ever *listens*?'

'Listens to what? Father never talks about anything but politics.' Elizabeth made a face. 'And politics is so boring.'

Virginia put her fists on her hips and shook her head at her sister. 'If you had the wit to pay attention to Father, you would realise that politics affect everything, Caro. And that includes you.'

* * *

Politics had no place in Tom's mind that summer of 1639. On any day when the weather was fair he went riding on his hobby-horse. He no longer sneaked away but marched boldly out the door, carrying his stick mount under his arm. After circling the house a time or two to make certain he was seen playing with his silly toy, he would gallop off. He abandoned the hobby-horse as soon as he was out of sight. It would remain hidden under a furze bush until he returned home. It had proved a good enough decoy, after all. The servants made jokes about his latest game. As soon as he was out of sight they forgot about him.

When Tom reached the cliff he would take off his shoes and stockings and roll up his breeches. Going barefoot was painful at first, but after a few days he could walk – even climb over rocks – without wincing.

Donal was often waiting for him at the cove with Maura. Although they never said so, Tom suspected they were as lonely for the company of other children as he was. If they did not appear he could spend hours watching the ever changing spectacle of the bay. Sometimes the water was cobalt blue. Or emerald green. Or even a clear, brilliant turquoise colour, streaked with royal purple.

He threw pebbles at seagulls. Searched for interesting

shells to collect for Maura. Lay on his back on the beach, gazing into the bottomless sky. Watching white-sailed galleons race before the wind. The ceaseless wind that blew over Roaringwater Bay.

One warm, muggy day Tom waded into the surf. The cold water swirling around his legs was wonderfully refreshing. He went farther out. Water to his hips. To his waist. Delicious.

Until a breaker swept him off his feet and into a roil of sand and stones and shells and seawater. As soon as he could stand up again he headed thankfully for the shore. Halfway there he stopped. Looked back at the water. He was wet anyway. Why not try?

Cautiously, Tom waded deeper. How do animals swim? Head above the water. Paddle with the front legs, kick with the back legs.

He took a deep breath and held it.

At first it seemed impossible. Then, to his surprise, he discovered he was swimming. Struggling, but staying up, not giving up. He opened his mouth to take a great gulp of much-needed air – and the sea poured in. Salty water flooded down his throat and up into his nasal passages. He was strangling.

Out of control and terrified, Tom thrashed violently in the water. And felt his toes graze the bottom.

Rowing backwards with his arms, he soon righted himself. The water came up to his chin but the bottom was still there, solid and reassuring. He was on a shelf that extended an unknown distance into the bay. As long as he went no further, he could practise swimming with confidence. If he remembered not to swallow any water.

By the time Tom returned to the beach his body felt well used, but his spirit was soaring. He promised himself he would swim every day he could.

He waited until his clothes were almost dry, then made his way home, eager for the next morning, when Donal and Maura might be there. And they were.

Tom did not talk about his newly acquired skill for fear they would want a demonstration. Instead he told them about life at Roaringwater House. Things that seemed commonplace to him fascinated them. When he described his bed-closet, Maura clapped her hands with delight. 'Tomflynn sleeps in a coffin!' she cried as she capered around him.

Tom had his own questions. 'How far back does the cave go, Donal?'

'Can you keep a secret?'

'I can.'

Donal led the other two into the cave. When their eyes grew accustomed to the darkness, he pointed out a narrow passageway leading to another chamber. 'Beyond this are more rooms,' he told Tom, 'but you'd want a torch to see them. We only carry one when it's needed.'

'What are the rooms used for?'

'Why do you think they're used for anything?'

Tom said, 'You told me your work was guarding the cave.'

'You have a good memory.'

'Ev'ryfink is used for somefink,' Maura volunteered.

Tom chuckled. 'Her English is not as good as yours, Donal, but she tries.'

'Our father insists we learn English so we can deal with the *Sasanach*,' said Donal. 'They're too thick to learn Irish,' he added scornfully.

'What dealings do you have with the *Sasanach*?'

Ignoring the question, Donal said, 'Only a few people know these caves are here. You can't see them unless you come right up to them. That's why they make such good storehouses.'

'Storehouses?' Tom queried. 'But they're empty.'

'They're empty now. The first time you were here they had casks of wine in them. Spanish sherry.'

'I don't understand, Donal.'

'I'm talking about making a living from the sea. That's what my family does. It isn't always sherry, either. Or port from Portugal. Sometimes it's swords, or silver, or Persian rugs. Once it was teeth.'

'Teeth!'

'Giant fangs,' said Donal. 'They were curved and white and longer than my leg. They came from Africa, so there must be giant wolves in Africa. I never want to go there, myself,' he added fervently.

Try as he might, Tom could not imagine wolves with fangs longer than a boy's leg. 'You're making that up, Donal.'

'I am not making it up. I swear on the Virgin.'

Tom only half believed the story about the fangs, but he was fascinated to learn of the wine. His father served port and sherry to his guests. Was he buying stolen goods without knowing it? Was Donal's family making a fool of William Flynn?

'Could I do what you do? Work with your family, maybe?' he asked Donal when they were out in the sunlight again.

'Are you serious?'

'I am serious,' Tom insisted. The idea had come to him in a rush. He could almost see himself carrying barrels in and out of the caves, whistling through his teeth, tossing his hair out of his eyes. Getting even with his father. 'Please, Donal. Give me a chance.'

The other boy looked doubtful. 'It's not for me to decide,' he said. 'You had best talk to my father.'

'Your father the king?'

'My father the king. I can tell him about your offer tonight. If he's interested, I'll take you to meet him tomorrow.'

Tom hardly slept that night. The morning dawned dark and stormy. By the time he was dressed the wind was howl-ing down the chimneys. It rattled the windows of the house and made the horses restless in the stable. When Tom came downstairs Elizabeth told him, 'Mother says you are not to go outside today.'

'I don't mind the weather. She thinks I'm still a baby.'

'She means it, Tom. You have to stay in.'

With a heavy heart, the boy went in search of a way to pass the time. He checked the traps in the cellar and released the rats. He tried to make them race one another but they ran away and hid instead. He then devoted himself to carving curlicues on the upstairs window frames – in places where no one would notice – with his penknife. Until the blade broke.

The storm grew worse. At midday the dairymaid complained to Cook that the cows in the dairy still had not let down their milk.

In the afternoon it seemed as if all of Roaringwater Bay was trying to come into the house. Tom had never been frightened of storms. They were both familiar and exciting. But this one was a giant. With giant fangs ...

He struggled to control his galloping imagination.

Catherine Flynn stayed in her room for most of the day. So did Elizabeth. Virginia busied herself trying to paint the storm, while Caroline painted beauty patches on her face with a bit of soot from the fireplace. Eventually Missus ordered the lamps to be lit and sent a housemaid to the cellar for more lamp oil. The housemaid returned to report that she could hear 'rats everywhere' and would not go down. In the end, Virginia went for the oil herself.

Night fell early. Darkness crept in through the windows and lay in inky pools on the floor. Tom's mother came downstairs to gather her children by the massive fireplace in the great hall. Mrs Flynn set to work darning a silk stocking. Every time the thunder rolled she flinched. Finally she laid aside the wooden darning egg and folded her hands in her lap.

Caroline paced nervously back and forth, picking up an ornament, setting it down again. Elizabeth and Virginia sat rigidly in their chairs, looking pale.

Tom longed to run upstairs and climb into his bed-closet and shut the panel tight. But he stayed where he was until the women went to bed.

The following morning the beach was littered with wreckage. Tangled masses of seaweed, driftwood, dead fish, broken shells. The sand stirred up from the bottom of the bay smelt rotten. But the sun shone. The sun shone! And Donal was waiting there for Tom.

• • • • • •

CHAPTER SIX

DUBLIN

The storm had blown itself out before reaching Dublin. The sky over the city was overcast but there was no mud in the streets, only horse dung and refuse. William Flynn paused to consult the new public clock on the Tholsel. Then he made his way toward Skinners' Row.

The city was growing, extending its boundaries. Land was rising in value day by day and week by week. The streets were crowded with gentlemen and beggars, foreigners and merchants and thieves. Almost every vessel that sailed into Dublin port brought more adventurers eager to make a fortune. The harbour was a veritable fortress of masts.

A new Custom House had been erected between Dame Street and the Liffey. Men of distinction were building fine homes along Wood Quay, replacing rotting wharves and warehouses. A new post office had opened in Castle Street.

Flynn's destination was a low building of red Dutch brick, which rubbed shoulders with a glovemaker's stall and a butchershop. When he pushed open the door, the smell of sweating male bodies was almost overpowering. Four men he knew were sitting at a heavy table near the door. He could not help noticing that they were drinking coffee instead of tea.

That is something else I was wrong about, Flynn thought glumly.

One of the men took a carved German pipe from his mouth long enough to call Flynn by name. Another pushed a stool forward with his booted foot. A large fellow with ginger whiskers said, 'Are you well, William?'

Flynn gave a wan smile. 'Well enough.'

'We did not expect to see you again so soon. What brings you back to the capital? Business as usual?'

'Pah!' Flynn sounded disgusted. 'Not this time. I have been seeking an interview with Richard Boyle.'

'Any success?'

'I waited all morning in his town house next to Dublin Castle. Magnificent place. Swarming with servants. One of them showed me to a room the size of a barn and left me there without even a drink in my hand. Every time I put my head out the door I was told the earl was busy.'

His friends exchanged meaningful glances.

'Oh, I saw the earl all right,' Flynn said bitterly. 'Saw him out the window as he drove away in a fine carriage – four perfectly matched greys and a man in crimson livery riding postillion. And not so much as a wave of his hand to me.

Order a coffee for me someone, please.' When a steaming bowl of coffee was placed before him he did not drink, but stared into the dark liquid as if seeing his future. 'It's the fourth time Boyle has avoided me, his soul to the devil. I cannot go cap-in-hand to him again.'

'Quite right too,' said Ginger Whiskers. 'A man has his pride.'

'Pride is a fine thing,' another remarked, 'if one can afford it.' He smoothed his hands across his plum-coloured waist-coat. 'William, you must remember that Richard Boyle is the richest man in Ireland now. He is hounded night and morning by petitioners. I dare say he is sick of the sight of pleading faces.'

An older man with a harsh voice like two stones scraping together said, 'Don't spare any sympathy for Boyle. Under-neath the fine feathers he is a scoundrel who is busy lining his own pockets at the expense of others. The Lord Deputy Thomas Wentworth is a better fellow altogether. He may not be the warmest man I ever met, but I would swear on my brother's life that Wentworth is honest. Which doesn't sit too well with Boyle, of course. If we have to choose sides, I choose Wentworth. Boyle has no respect for the king and no real feeling for the people.'

William Flynn looked deeply worried. 'My family lost their lands in the Elizabethan War,' he said. 'I have only a few acres I inherited from an uncle. A political appointment would enable me to protect them. One word from an influential friend was all I needed to get my toes under the government table in Dublin. Instead ... ' He sagged on the stool. 'Instead, I have called the wolf into the fold.'

Plum Waistcoat leaned forward and licked his lips with interest. 'Really? How?'

'By inviting Richard Boyle to Roaringwater House. I boasted of the fine estate I had created out of nothing. He was impressed, all right. He decided then and there to extend the plantation of Munster and grab the land for his favourites.' William Flynn's voice dropped to a shamed whisper. 'And in my confusion ... in my craven fear of his power ... I offered to help.'

'You poor fool,' said Ginger Whiskers. 'You might as well have handed him the deeds to your land.'

Pipe Smoker studied his smouldering tobacco. 'Perhaps you should apply to Thomas Wentworth instead.'

'Waste of breath,' declared Plum Waistcoat. 'The interests of the Crown are all the Lord Deputy cares about. He runs roughshod over everyone else in the name of King Charles.'

Harsh Voice said, 'The king needs all the support he can get. In spite of his efforts on their behalf, the Catholics still don't trust him. The Puritans hate him, the Scots have rebelled and there's war looming between Charles and the English parliament.'

'Meanwhile here in Ireland Wentworth and Boyle are

fighting each other,' Ginger Whiskers pointed out. 'The Lord Deputy decided to make an example of Boyle for defrauding the Crown. He fined the earl fifteen thousand pounds for questionable practices in the diocese of Lismore. He also forced him to move the elaborate family tomb he had built in the heart of St Patrick's Cathedral. Now it gathers dust in a side aisle.'

'Wentworth has made a bitter enemy of the Earl of Cork,' Plum Waistcoat warned. 'Boyle will turn the entire government against him. And he knows just which strings to pull, which debts to call in. Boyle has a whole string of money-lenders working for him, you know. He's even loaned money to King Charles.'

Pipe Smoker summed up the situation. 'There are bad times ahead, my friends. Bad times indeed. I advise you to keep your heads below the parapet. We are merely pawns in larger games.'

William Flynn looked around the table. Nobody said anything. After a while he got up and left the coffee house.

'There goes a desperate man,' Harsh Voice remarked as the door closed behind him.

'These are desperate times,' said Ginger Whiskers.

* * *

Leaving the cove behind, Donal led Tom along the coast. The waters of the bay were still rough. Great breakers deposited mountains of foam and scud wherever they touched land. Ragged clouds raced across an otherwise blue sky. There were several places where Tom tried to stop for a moment and enjoy the view. Donal, who had seen it all many times before, trotted on. Tom had to run to catch up with him.

Tom felt a growing excitement. He had never met a king before. Even his father had never met a king, though William Flynn spoke of King Charles as if he were a personal friend.

At its best the way was rough and broken. The boys climbed up and down steep slopes and made their way along the crumbling edges of unstable cliffs, where the ground threatened to collapse beneath their feet at any moment. Caught between sea and sky, they moved through a magical, ever-shifting light that made it impossible to judge distances.

'Mind you keep an eye on the path,' warned Donal.

'I don't see any path.'

Donal laughed. He was as agile as a wild goat. Tom twice skinned his knees and once narrowly avoided breaking his ankle. 'Do we have far to go?' he panted.

'Not very,' Donal assured him. 'It only seems like a long way because you're not used to it.'

Tom had just about decided to turn around when Donal announced, 'Here we are.'

Ahead lay a marshy area studded with clumps of willow bushes like miniature islands. Through this wetland a little river emptied into the bay. The stream flowed sleepily along, in no hurry to reach the sea. By contrast the willows were bristling with energy. Wind trailed long fingers through their branches, turning the slender leaves first to show their brilliant green side, then reversing to silver. Shining waves of green and silver followed one another in constant motion.

Tom was entranced by the sight. He almost failed to notice that Donal had turned inland to follow the course of the river. He had to run to catch up.

As they followed a footbeaten track along the riverbank the sound of the bay gradually receded into the distance. The air grew very still.

In the reedy shallows a solitary heron waited, immobile, to spear an unsuspecting fish. The bird was so involved in its task it did not blink as the boys walked past.

When they came to a bend in the river Donal's pace increased. Tom felt his own heart beat faster.

A short distance beyond the bend, steep hills rose on either side of a narrow valley. Nestled in the valley was a handful of stone cabins whitewashed with lime. They had been built with their backs to a hill and their fronts to the sun. Their roofs were thatched with reeds securely pegged down. A round, stone bake-oven stood at a safe distance from the dwellings. Between the cabins and the river Tom saw a clutter of lobster pots and fishing nets and coils of rope and upside-down currachs. And other articles whose use he could not guess.

For a moment he thought he heard his father's warning: A fate worse than death!

Donal gave him a shove from behind. 'Go on,' he urged. 'They're waiting for you.'

In front of the largest cabin a woman sat at a spinning wheel. She was humming as she worked. Maura was leaning against her shoulder. The two looked up as the boys approached. 'Tomflynn!' the little girl shouted. She ran to meet him with arms outstretched. 'Tomflynn, Tomflynn!'

A man appeared in the doorway behind the woman. She looked back at him. He briefly rested one hand on her hair.

People began to emerge from the other cabins. Four men – one of them quite old – a woman well past her youth, and another in her middle years. Seeing them together, Tom understood the meaning of 'tribe'. Men and women alike were tall and strongly built. All but the oldest had thick black hair. Everyone, even little Maura, possessed the same bright blue eyes and sharply cut features.

They were nothing like the people William Flynn entertained at Roaringwater House. Tom recalled his father's guests with a newly critical eye. Their faces resembled suet puddings. Their clothes were too tight and their bellies were too big.

On Roaringwater Bay lived a tribe with the faces of sea eagles.

The man standing in the doorway wore a saffron-dyed linen tunic and woollen trews. His feet were clad in untanned leather that softly fitted their shape. Slung across his broad shoulders was a mantle trimmed in wolf fur.

Tom had no doubt who he was. Donal's father looked more like a king than Charles Stuart in his ermines.

How does one greet a king?

Donal's father solved the problem for Tom by stepping forward and putting one hand on the boy's shoulder. The man's eyes sparkled with some hidden amusement. 'I am chieftain here,' Muiris said. 'And you are the son of Liam Ó Floinn.' Not a question, but a statement. 'Does your father know where you are?'

'My father doesn't care what I do, as long as I stay out of his sight.'

'Donal says you would like to work with us. Is that true, Tomás?'

It was strange to hear his name pronounced in the Irish way. The servants at home would never dare. 'It is true,' said Tom. 'Learning about the sea would be a great adventure.'

'It might be,' Muiris conceded. 'Is adventure your only reason?' He cocked one black eyebrow. His blue eyes seemed to see right through Tom.

The boy hesitated. How could he admit that he wanted

to get back at his father? 'If do have another reason,' he said, 'must I tell you what it is?'

Muiris shook his head. 'I have no need for your secrets. It is enough that you know them.'

CHAPTER SEVEN

IN THE NARROW VALLEY

the chieftain's hand on Tom's shoulder guaranteed the boy's acceptance. Muiris introduced the others. His wife was called Bríd. Two of the men, Seán and Séamus, were his brothers. The younger woman was married to Séamus and the older to his cousin.

'Tomás. Tomás. You are very welcome, Tomás,' said voices on every side.

There was a rush to offer the visitor hospitality. He was led into a thick-walled cabin and seated on a three-legged stool close to the hearth. He gazed at his surroundings with interest.

Rectangular in shape, the cabin was more spacious than it appeared from the outside. The wide, deep hearth was the heart of the home. Its stone chimney soared to the full height of the roofline. Recesses in the chimney breast provided storage. Cooking pots were slung on an iron crane over the slumbering hearthfire. Against one wall stood a large timber dresser. Its shelves were filled with pewter cups and plates and the imported Dutch pottery called 'delft', after the city where it was made. Underneath this was a nesting box for the hens.

At one end of the main room a wooden ladder led to the children's sleeping loft under the eaves. A partition at the other end separated their parents' bedroom from the rest of the house. Windows on either side of the door provided daylight for both the main room and the bedroom. Everything the family needed was snugly contained under one roof.

Donal's family gathered around Tom. He was not used to being the centre of favourable attention. When they pressed food and drink upon him he refused nothing. The spoons were made of mussel shells with bowls that looked like pearls.

Tom ate things with legs, and squishy things, and things with eyes on stalks – because Donal was eating them too. After a while he realised they were delicious. When he was offered a drink which smelled like honey and seaweed, he choked on the first swallow. As soon as he could draw breath again, he laughed. The others laughed with him. After a while he held out his cup for more.

When the younger woman began to sing Tom did not understand all the words. But the music rang in his blood and bones.

He felt at ease with Donal's family from the beginning. They did not talk to him as if he were a child, and they listened when he spoke, as if he were an adult.

Donal's mother wanted to hear about Roaringwater House. 'You amaze me,' she said after Tom had described the house for her in detail. 'A special room just for sitting, and others for eating and sewing and even dressing! Would you not dress beside your bed, Tomás?'

'My father says a dressing room is an English custom.'

'Ah, English,' she said. 'I myself was reared in an earthen hovel with one little room for the nine of us and a stall at the end for the cow – when we had a cow. A damp, dark place it was, on the edge of a bog. My poor mother and five of her children coughed their lives away there. The feet of misfortune walked in the tracks of my family. Then one day Muiris found me at the market, Tomás, trying to sell a few pitiful herbs.' Suddenly Bríd clapped her hands and laughed, as if to blow sorrow away. 'And here I am!' Her smile was so bright he had to smile back.

Nothing more was said about Tom's request to be part of their work. He did not press the point. It was enough to be here. He stayed with Donal's people until a change in the light warned him it was time to go home.

But already the community in the narrow valley felt like home to him.

As he was leaving, the old woman caught his arm and

pulled him aside. In a hoarse whisper she said, 'What is for you will not pass by you.'

Much later, as Tom lay in his bed, he looked back on the day with astonishment. He felt like a chick who had broken out of its egg.

The following morning brought gale force winds and hammering rain. Tom went from window to window, peering out anxiously. He was afraid his father would come home soon and demand to know how he was spending his time. If he does, Tom told himself, I'll run away. I'll go to live with Donal and never come back.

Around noon the skies cleared, leaving the land fresh-washed and fragrant. Tom and his hobby-horse were out the door at once. He hurried to hide the horse, then ran to the cliffs. To Tom's surprise it was not Donal waiting for him in the cove. It was Muiris.

He sat in a small currach that bobbed in the shallows. When he saw Tom he vaulted out of the boat. The boy watched in open-mouthed admiration as Muiris, thigh deep in the foaming tide, effortlessly lifted the currach, flipped it over and waded ashore, carrying his boat on his back like the shell of a black beetle.

Setting the currach down on the beach, he asked, 'Are you well, Tomás?'

'I am well. And yourself?'

'I am always well,' Muiris replied. 'And how is your mother?'

The question was unexpected. 'My mother is well enough,
I suppose. She's never very strong,' the boy added truthfully.

'It is sorry I am to hear that. Does she have enough food?'

'We have more than enough food,' Tom assured Muiris.
'My mother has only a small appetite, but my father never
lets her want for anything.'

'He is not a *sprissaun*, then,' Muiris said in a low voice,
almost as if he were talking to himself.

'What is a *sprissaun*?'

'A person of no value,' the man replied.

'That does not apply to my father,' said Tom. 'My father ...'
the boy struggled to find the right words. He was not used to
defending William Flynn. 'My father does his best.'

'Which is all a man can do,' Muiris told him. 'Now we
must talk about you, Tomás, and the possibility of working
with us.' Donal's father smiled then, though not with his lips.
The smile was in his eyes. 'Did my son explain what we do?'

'He said you make your living from the sea. At first I
thought he meant you were sailors. I liked the idea of being
a sailor. Then I realised my mistake. In some way your work
involves caves as well as ships.'

Muiris did not agree or disagree. 'The ships that travel
around our coast carry ore and timber and salt,' he said
evenly. 'How do you connect that to caves?'

'Ships can carry wine, too,' replied the boy. 'And even giant
teeth, according to Donal.'

Muiris grinned unexpectedly, his whole face lighting up. 'My son has a vivid imagination. And you have a clever head, Tomás. You already have put some of the pieces together. You see, King Charles is a greedy man. He has placed huge customs duties on goods brought into Ireland. His tax collectors meet cargo vessels at the dock. But suppose part of a shipment is offloaded at night before the ships reach port?'

Tom's stomach did a back flip. 'You are pirates!'

'Not a bit of it, lad. We are smugglers, which is a safer job of work. I have a wife and children to think of, and no smuggler has yet been hanged in Ireland.'

'But ... I thought ... are there any pirates around here?'

'Indeed there are, lad; Turks and Algerians and others as well. Wherever you find the sea you find pirates. One of the greatest Gaelic families used to be the terror of the southern coast. My own sept, however, is too small for—'

'Sept?'

'A sept is a branch of a much larger clan,' Muiris explained. 'Our sept has only a few men now, we lost some to fever and some to the sea. Because of the pirates, English warships patrol the shipping routes these days. Most merchantmen are supplied with matchlocks and pistols. We avoid such problems by making a business arrangement ahead of time.'

Tom was both frightened and intrigued. As usual, curiosity won out. 'What sort of arrangement?'

'Nothing that need concern you, Tomás,' Muiris replied.

'Are you certain you want to do this?'

Tom knew he could walk away. He did not understand why Muiris was willing to let him join them at all. But he did not want to walk away. Nothing so thrilling had ever happened to him before. 'I am certain,' he said.

'If I should summon you at night, could you come to this cove?'

'After I go to bed they forget about me. I can sneak out without being seen, any time I want. But how will you summon me?'

'Your house has only a few small windows on the side nearest the bay. There is one with solid timber shutters near the corner of the second storey.'

'That's my bed-chamber! How do you know about it?'

'From that window you should be able to see a signal light,' Muiris continued without answering Tom's question. 'If we need you, there will be two flashes of light shortly after sundown. As soon as you see them, count to five. Then you will see three more. That means come down to the beach as soon as you can. A boat will be waiting for you.'

A boat will be waiting for you. Tom hugged himself with excitement. He had never been in a boat.

Muiris said, 'A cargo vessel will drop anchor at a pre-arranged place in the bay. We – you and my other men – will row out to meet it.'

My other men!

'We will load goods from the ship into our boat while the captain and crew look the other way. Then we will bring the merchandise ashore and hide it in these caves. In time other men will come for it.'

'Where do they take it? Do they sell it? Who buys the—'

'Donal warned me that you would ask a lot of questions,' Muiris interrupted. 'I have just told you all you need to know. Now, and for the last time – do you still want to join us?'

* * *

William Flynn returned to Roaringwater House in a black mood. The long ride from Dublin, attended only by a groom for the horses, had exhausted him. His worries rode with him and gave him no peace. When the two men stopped for the night at various inns along the way, his bed was always damp, his meal tasteless. He suspected the groom was more comfortable than he, sleeping in a dry stable.

At last the house he had built with such high hopes lay before him. He drew rein abruptly. The groom was so close behind that his horse ran into the haunches of his master's horse. Flynn's bay gelding pinned his ears back and tried to kick the other animal.

William Flynn swore at all of them.

He slouched in the saddle and stared at his house. His mansion. From a distance it looked perfect, gilded by the last rays of the setting sun. But he knew it was not perfect. Every chimney smoked and every room was draughty, no matter how many tapestries he hung over the cracks in the walls. There was a distinct smell of mould in the kitchen. The plaster on the ceiling of Elizabeth's bed-chamber was beginning to peel away. There was a leak in the roof too, somewhere. There was always a leak in the roof somewhere.

The land on which the house stood was no better. The soil was thin and stony, breaking the backs and the hearts of the few tenants who tried to farm it. There was never enough grass for horses and dairy cows and barely enough for sheep. He could no longer sell the wool anyway. Export duties were too high.

I should give the whole place to the first man who asks for it, Flynn thought to himself. But I would rather die than lose any part of it.

When he stomped into the hall in his filthy boots, the first person he saw was Tom.

The boy gave him a startled look. 'You're back! I mean–'

'Did you hope I would never return, you pitiful lout? You were wrong. This is my home, begog, built with my own blood and sweat. What have you ever contributed? Nothing!'

Tom took a step backwards to avoid his father's exploding temper. 'I'm glad you're home, sir, truly I am, we have all mi–'

'Don't lie to me, boy!' As he spoke, Flynn was fumbling with the ties of his travelling cloak. He threw off the garment and flung it to the floor. 'Why are you still dressed?' he demanded to know. 'The sun is down, you should be in your nightshirt and out of my sight!'

Tom hurried for the stairs.

The boy had formed the habit of keeping his clothes on until the first stars appeared. Every evening he watched for the signal from Muiris. It had not come yet, but it must do soon.

His father's arrival made Tom more eager than ever to put distance between himself and Roaringwater House.

He raced up the stairs and into his chamber. Two strides took him to the window. Throwing open the timber shutters, he gazed towards the bay. Soon he saw two flashes of light. Heart pounding, he counted to five. There were three more flashes. Tom took off his shoes and stuffed his stockings into them. Carrying the shoes in his hand, he slipped from his room. He quietly made his way to the back staircase. If one of the servants saw him he would try to talk his way out of trouble.

Fortunately he met no one. Down the stairs, along the passage, out the rear door, across the stable yard, around the dovecote, past the dairy, past the kitchen garden, the poultry house and the midden heap ... he ran until his lungs were bursting. Ran towards the familiar outcrop of furze at the edge of the cliff.

In deepening twilight he picked his way among the rocks

which marked the narrow downward path. Until he reached
the foot of the cliff Tom could not tell if anyone was in the
cove. To his vast relief, the same currach he had seen before
was waiting in the shallows. This time Séamus was at the oars.
The boy asked, 'Where is Muiris?'

'My brother will be meeting us at the mouth of our river,'
Séamus replied, 'with a larger boat to carry cargo. Get in
now.'

'Just a moment.' Tom ran to the cave and tucked his shoes
and stockings inside. Then he waded into the shallows and
tried to climb into the currach.

Getting in was not as easy as it looked. The little boat was
as skittish as a nervous horse. When it felt his weight it tilted
violently to one side.

Séamus laughed. 'Easy, lad. Do not lunge at her, come up
easy, like. Slip over the side like an eel over a tree root.' He
leaned away from Tom to balance the boat, and the boy tried
again.

'Easy, like,' Tom muttered under his breath.

After two more embarrassing attempts he finally managed
to get in without overturning the currach. Aside from leaning, Séamus had done nothing to help him. 'Sit still now,' he
instructed. He took up the oars and began to row. 'Watch
what I do, lad. Ye might do this yourself some day.'

Tom gave the pair of oars a hard look. They were very
long and narrow, with a flat blade at the end instead of a

paddle. He could not imagine them propelling a boat forward. But when skilfully handled by Séamus, they made the small currach seem to fly over the water.

CHAPTER EIGHT

ROARINGWATER BAY

'**M**r Fox has not called on you since the betrothal party,' William Flynn said accusingly. 'What have you done to upset him, Elizabeth?'

'How could I upset him if I have not seen him?'

'You must encourage your suitor more, my girl. You don't have so many danglers you can afford to let this one get away.'

'I accepted his offer of marriage, Father, what more do you want?'

Flynn could no longer restrain himself, even with one of his beloved daughters. 'It is woman's work to keep the pot on the boil! You should have been writing frequent letters to Herbert Fox, assuring him of your undying devotion. Scenting the letters with some of the expensive perfume I gave you. Must I think of everything myself? The lot of you hang out of me like leeches. Taking and taking, never giving!'

Elizabeth ran crying to her mother. 'I've done everything Father asked of me, always. Still he wants more. Is there no pleasing him?'

Lying half submerged in the pile of pillows on her bed, Catherine Flynn turned a pale face towards her daughter. Elizabeth bent low to hear her words.

'What did William ask of you now?'

'To embroider some flags for Mr Fox's ships. I'm not artistic, Mother, you know I'm not. My embroidery is pitiful. Ginny should be doing this. Then I could say it was mine.'

'That would not be honest, dear. You would be deceiving the man who has promised to marry you.'

'What difference would that make? Have you always told Father everything?'

Mrs Flynn said, 'William knows all there is to know about me.' Her whispery voice faded to a mere thread. 'Yet he loves me anyway.'

Elizabeth stood at her mother's bedside, looking down. 'Of course he does, Mother. You are beautiful.'

Catherine Flynn gave a hollow laugh.

* * *

The rhythmic sound of the oars ... *tloc swoosh, tloc swoosh, tloc swoosh* ... accompanied the little boat like a kind of music. Séamus stayed close to the shore. Tom relaxed and began to enjoy himself.

He was careful to watch how Séamus handled the oars.

Travelling in a boat, he decided, was easier and more

81

pleasant than travelling on land. Riding the waves. He could imagine himself making other, longer voyages. Perhaps some day he might even sail to the New World.

Come and take a ride with me upon my magic pony, fast and far we'll travel all the live long day …

As night took hold, the sky above the bay was losing its peacock radiance. There was no visible moon.

They reached the mouth of the little river more quickly than he had expected. Muiris, Seán and Fergal, the younger of the two male cousins, were waiting with a much larger currach. 'Isn't Donal coming?' Tom asked.

'Donal is still a boy,' said Muiris. 'Strong and willing surely, but what we do tonight is man's work.'

Man's work. Tom wished his father could hear those words.

Transferring into the larger boat was another challenge. No one offered to help him this time. He was directed to sit in the middle of the boat. 'I don't suppose you know how to row?' Seán asked.

'Not yet,' said Tom.

'Not yet,' Muiris echoed. 'D'ye hear him, lads? He has a head on his shoulders, this one. Tomás knows he is for the rowing.'

Séamus stood knee deep in water to shove the currach forward, then vaulted over the side and took a place in the stern. The drumbeat of oars with four men rowing was like a mighty heartbeat.

The waves came to meet them.

In common with all currachs, the boat was made of hides stretched over a light but sturdy frame of wickerwork. It was large enough to transport a grown cow from one island to another. As flexible as a living creature, the currach adapted to every wave.

Tom had watched his father's head groom break colts to the saddle. The young horses leaped and plunged, but the head groom clung to them like a burr. He made it look easy. As the currach began to leap and plunge Tom realised it was not easy. His head knew he was in no danger of falling, but his stomach had a different opinion.

'Sit easy, lad,' Muiris said out of the side of his mouth. 'Do not fight the motion, ride with it.'

Tom followed his advice. Soon he was grinning into the wind. His eyes adjusted to the darkness. The water seemed to give off a faint light of its own, as if reflecting the vanished day.

He had not brought a warm coat because he had never seen the others wearing warm coats. It was cold on the bay after the sun went down, but he loved it. The pitch sealing the seams of the oxhide had a sharp smell that caught in the back of his throat. He loved it.

At night Roaringwater Bay seemed larger than ever. Wave upon heaving wave rolled away towards the end of the world. Tom could not tell where the boat was in relation to the land. If the land was still out there. Perhaps it had disappeared entirely, and he would ride the cresting waves in the company of these men forever.

He loved it.

When he saw a dark bulk looming off to one side he knew they were passing an island. Soon a small red glow appeared to the other side.

'There she is,' Seán announced. 'I see the captain's lamp.'

The oarsmen adjusted their direction.

'Sit easy, Tomás,' Muiris said again. 'You are not going aboard this time.'

This time!

'Stay in the boat with Séamus and Fergal to receive our cargo. Séamus will show you how to distribute the load evenly in the bottom of the boat. It is important to keep a currach stable.'

Tom had seen sailing ships only at a distance. He had no idea of their true size. As the currach drew alongside, he had to tilt his head back to look up as far as the gunwales. He had expected great sails towering overhead, yards and yards of billowing canvas like the clouds that sailed above the bay. But the sails were lowered. The wind whistled through the shrouds.

Tom was awestruck. 'That ship is enormous!'

Séamus laughed. 'You think that's big? She's only a little Portuguese caravel out of Lisbon.'

'How can you tell?'

'Easy enough. She has a square-rigged foremast raked well forward, with a foresail and topsail and a spritsail over the bows. That high stern is to keep her from being over-whelmed by following seas when she's sailing before the wind. Her flags tell her nationality and home port.'

'Oh,' said Tom.

A rope ladder was thrown down from above. Muiris and Seán scrambled up with marvellous agility and disappeared over the rail. The others waited below.

Tom was aware of the bulk of the ship looming above him. The caravel had a voice of its own. It groaned and muttered like an old man who could not get comfortable in his bed. From somewhere deep in its bowels came a rumbling noise.

Time passed. The men waiting in the currach heard human voices above them, though they could not make out the words. Someone held a lantern aloft and peered over the side. The light lasted only for a few moments before it was withdrawn.

More time passed. Then – 'Ready below?' Muiris called down.

'Ready,' Séamus answered crisply.

A loaded cargo net was swung over the side of the ship and lowered, swinging, toward the water. Séamus and Fergal prepared to pull it into the boat. Tom was faster. He leaped to his feet and tried to catch hold of the net himself.

The currach promptly rolled sideways, in the direction of the waiting ship. Tom frantically cartwheeled his arms in the air to regain his balance.

He failed.

The icy water waited below. The caravel was so close it looked like crushing him. He tried to throw himself back into the boat, but his weight was too far committed in the other direction. He felt himself going, going ....

A strong hand caught him by the back of his collar and pulled him to safety.

'*Amadán!*' scolded Fergal. 'What are you doing at all?'

'Trying to help,' Tom panted.

'You can help by following instructions. Sit down there and wait,' said Séamus.

Tom sat.

The two men eased the loaded cargo net into the middle of the boat. When it was settled, Fergal whistled two short notes. The lantern was held over the rail again. 'Is there any more?' Fergal called up.

'One more. Mind yourselves now.'

'Sit still, Tomás,' Séamus repeated, unnecessarily. Tom was folded in upon himself, too ashamed to move.

When the second net reached the currach the two men settled it behind the first. Séamus told Tom, 'Ease towards the stern now while we open the nets.'

Tom needed all of his courage to obey. The slightest movement of the currach made his stomach turn over. When he reached the stern, Séamus said, 'I will hand you boxes from one of the nets. Arrange them in the bottom of the boat. The lightest in the front, the heavier ones behind.'

In near darkness, Tom obeyed. The boxes were of different shapes and sizes. Some rattled when he lifted them. 'What's in these?'

'Spices and palm oil,' said Fergal, 'from the West Indies. We have jugs of black rum, too. They go in the centre of the boat.'

'What is black rum?'

'The sweetest drink you could ever taste, Tomás, except you won't be tasting this lot. Neither will the men who are expecting it. Their shipment seems to have come up short.'

The two men cackled with laughter.

When the nets were empty and their contents stowed in the currach, Fergal gave another sharp whistle. Unseen hands hauled the empty nets back up to the deck of the ship. Moments later, Muiris and Seán climbed down the rope ladder and into their boat.

'Good job, lads,' Muiris remarked as they rowed away from the ship.

Tom expected Séamus to tell his brother about Tom's disobedience. When he said nothing, the boy threw him a grateful glance – which Séamus could not see in the dark.

After a few minutes Tom remarked, 'You didn't really need

me, Muiris. You had enough men already.'

'Enough for this job, perhaps, but there will be other times when we do need help. It is important that you have experience.'

'I've had plenty of experience tonight,' Tom said truthfully.

The currach travelled on. Ploughing the rough sea, under the silent stars.

'Did you pay the captain?' Fergal asked Muiris.

'I did, of course. I paid him exactly what we had agreed. He thought he should have more, but ...'

'You made him think again.'

'I made him think again,' said Muiris. 'We will have a nice profit out of this night's work.'

Tom spoke up. 'If you paid him, it wasn't robbery.'

'Of course it was not robbery,' Muiris said. He sounded insulted. 'It was business. Though I grant you, it can be hard to tell the difference. Some ship captains are honest. Others, like the one on that caravel, are corrupt to the bone. They skim their ship's supplies and sell the goods ashore, or keep the ship undermanned and pocket the money that is meant to hire a larger crew. And it is not always the captain who is dishonest. Sometimes it is the owner. There are many ways in which the owner of a ship, or a fleet of ships, can enrich himself and no one the wiser. Och, Tomás, we have many partners in our business.'

* * *

William Flynn stood in the doorway of his wife's bed-chamber. 'Are you awake? The hour is late, but–'

'I am usually awake, even at this hour,' replied a soft voice from the darkness. 'Is something wrong, William?'

'I fear I must return to Dublin.' He went to sit beside her on the bed. 'I should never have left the capital when I did. I let myself be discouraged and gave in, which is not like me.'

'No, dear,' she agreed, moving over to make more room for him.

'I hesitate to tell you this because I do not want to worry you, Kate. Strangers have been asking questions in Bantry about the size of my property. Unless I act quickly, the bailiffs may throw us off our land and give it to the New English.'

His wife gave a muffled cry of distress.

He swiftly gathered her into his arms. 'Don't be frightened, Kate,' he murmured. ''Pon my honour, I vow no one will take your home from you.'

'How can you prevent it?'

'By following the advice I was given,' he replied. 'I shall call on the Lord Deputy, Thomas Wentworth, in Dublin Castle. Beg him on bended knee if I must. My desire for a political appointment is not merely selfish ambition; it is a matter of survival. If I have a position with the administration I can protect my property.'

'Are you certain?'

'I am not certain of anything any more,' Flynn said gloomily.

She forgot her own distress. 'Oh my dear, this will mean another dreadfully long ride for you.'

'Not this time. In the interest of haste, I shall ride to Cobh and book passage on a ship from there.' He forced a smile. 'We are about to have a ship owner in the family, remember? Might as well make use of him.'

CHAPTER NINE

• • • • • • •

SUMMER STORM

Afterwards Tom could hardly believe his adventure. He was safely back in his bed by the time the sun was up. The night had passed as swiftly as a dream. But he had proof of his exploits. His damp clothing, still smelling of salt and pitch, was wadded up in a corner of his room.

Tucked under his goosedown pillow were several small, tightly wrapped packets. Muiris had given them to him when they parted. 'Thank you for the night's work, Tomás. You are entitled to a share of the proceeds.'

When Tom unwrapped one of the packets he found a number of small brown stones. He was puzzled. 'Why are you giving me pebbles?'

Muiris chuckled. 'Not pebbles, lad. Whole nutmegs. Those other packets contain cloves and mace and cinnamon, as well as saffron and ginger. Spices have become very costly because of the import duties. If you sell yours in the village markets you can make quite a bit of money – just don't mention where you got them. Better still, keep them. A pinch of spice in your mother's food may tempt her appetite.'

'It's kind of you to care about my mother's welfare.'

Muiris cocked one eyebrow. 'Some say I am a kind man, Tomás.'

As soon as Tom had washed his face in the basin on his washstand and dressed in fresh clothes, he went down to the kitchen. He found Cook pummelling a large ball of dough. He stood watching for several moments, savouring the yeasty smell. Then he took a folded square of paper from his pocket and laid it on the table. 'This is to season Mother's food,' he said.

Cook frowned at him. 'Are you playing another of your pranks, Master Thomas?'

'I am not. Truly.'

Unfolding the paper, Cook found a small quantity of red powder. She lowered her head and sniffed. 'Cinnamon! And richer than the stuff that costs a fortune in Bantry. Where did this come from?'

'A friend gave it to me as a gift for Mother,' Tom said casually. He was thankful that servants were discouraged from asking questions. 'Do you think she will like it? If she does, I have this for her, and this too.' He produced several other papers.

When Cook sniffed the nutmeg her eyes lit up. 'The very thing for making a hot posset, and myself knowing Walter Raleigh's own secret recipe for sack posset,' she boasted.

'A secret? Can you tell me? Please?'

'You're a bit of a dark horse, Master Thomas. You're a great one for the eating but I never knew you were interested in the cooking.'

Tom grinned. 'I'm interested in a lot of things. You would be surprised.'

'Hmmph,' she said, 'I've reared seven childer of me own. Nothing about young ones surprises me any more. But I'll tell you, so I will. Because you said please.

'First boil together half a pint of sack sherry and half a pint of ale. Take the pot away from the fire and stir in a quart of hot cream – not boiled, mind, just scalding. And stir slow. Sweeten the mixture with lots of honey and grated nutmeg, then pour it into a well-warmed pewter bowl. And there you have it, Master Thomas.' She beamed with pride. 'The drink that gave the famous Raleigh his strength. 'Twill surely do our poor lady a power of good.'

While Cook prepared and served the posset, Tom avoided his father. William Flynn was about to leave for Dublin again. The boy did not join his sisters at the door to wave goodbye. Instead he went upstairs to see if his mother had drunk the hot posset. The pewter bowl on the candle stand beside her bed was empty and she was sleeping peacefully. Perhaps there was even a little colour in her cheeks?

Perhaps not.

Clouds were gathering over the bay. The wind brought a smell of rain.

* * *

Later in the day Tom grew restless. The gathering storm was making him jumpy. His mother had retired to her room and his sisters were busy with their own amusements. Roaring-water House crouched sullenly on its ground while every gust of wind sent more draughts billowing through the large, high-ceilinged rooms.

Tom did not expect to be summoned that night. The weather was too threatening. There was nothing for it but to remain inside and imagine a different, better life.

Donal and Maura would be sitting by their hearth, warm and snug, surrounded by loving family. The children might be helping their mother card wool or listening to someone tell stories. Muiris was a great one for relating history, but Seán was better at the legends of ancient Ireland. His words could bring to life the grim Fomorians who had built giant stone fortresses along the western coast; the beautiful and magical Tuatha dé Danann who could control the wind and weather; the aristocratic Milesians whose iron swords had driven the Tuatha dé Danann underground – or caused them to turn themselves into thorn trees.

And Seán's wife could sing haunting songs of the Gaelic

past that brought tears to the eyes.

Why is there no music in this house? Tom wondered. In the great hall there was a fine old harp which his mother used to play, or so she said. He had never heard her playing it. The elaborately carved body of the instrument was usually dusty and the strings were tarnished. When he ran his fingers across them they gave off a shrill whine.

The wind rose with a shrill whine.

* * *

At the first rumble of thunder Maura climbed onto her mother's lap. 'Make it go away,' she pleaded. She had been practising her English recently, so she could talk to Tomflynn better.

'Only God can do that, *girsha*.'

'You were praying to Him just now. I saw your lips move. Ask Him to make it go away.'

Bríd twined the child's silky curls around her fingers. 'I am asking Him for too much already,' she said. 'I am praying for the lives of all the people on the sea today. That is a fierce storm coming. Ships may be blown onto the rocks, or over-turned by the gale, and the poor people will struggle in the water, choking and gasping, until it pulls them down. Och, that is a terrible death!'

Maura pulled free of her mother's caress. 'Why do people

95

be on ships?' she asked reasonably.

'Some men cannot stay in one place forever, like a tree on its roots,' Bríd explained. 'The need for movement is in them. Ships take them where they could not go on their feet.'

'They should stay home,' Maura declared with conviction.

From the other side of the hearth Donal said, 'If he did not go smuggling, would our father stay home?'

'He would not, and why should he? My husband is a warrior like his father's fathers. He would go into the mountains and join the rebel chieftains.'

Donal's eyes sparkled with excitement. 'Would he be fighting the *Sasanach* then?'

'Muiris is fighting the *Sasanach* now,' Bríd replied calmly.

Maura said, 'The stuff he takes is worth a lot of money. He hurts the *Sasanach* somefin' awful, 'cos they love money more than anyfing.'

Her mother's shoulders shook with laughter.

Muiris entered the cabin, brushing the rain from his clothes. 'Why are you laughing?'

His wife said, 'Your daughter has the clearest eyes of any of us.'

'I know that,' he replied as he bent down and gathered Maura into his arms. 'When I need someone to tell me the truth, I ask this little one.'

* * *

As it always did, the storm finally blew itself out. The following day was gilded with late summer. Deep blue water reflected deep blue sky. The formerly furious wind was peacefully employed in filling the sails of countless vessels. They glided across the bay and around the coast of Ireland.

As he drew near the cliffs, Tom squinted to see better. Even the nearest small boat was too far away for him to recognise the occupants. The great ships that braved the trade routes from Africa and Spain were no more than dots on the horizon. He wondered if one of them would be waiting at Cobh when his father arrived.

Would there be pirates lurking along the way?

Tom was almost sorry Muiris was not a pirate. He could imagine the two men facing one another on the deck of a ship. William Flynn would lose all his bluster then. Muiris would not hurt him – of course not! – but he would make him feel helpless. Perhaps Muiris would even say, 'Tomás is my man now.'

Donal was not waiting in the cove. Sure of his welcome, Tom struck out for the settlement in the valley. He found Donal and Maura beside the river, scrubbing a cooking pot with sand. 'Tomflynn!' the little girl cried when she saw him. 'Did you hear the storm last night, Tomflynn?'

'It was ferocious,' he replied.

'F'rocious,' she agreed. 'I hate thumble.'

'She means thunder,' explained Donal.

Maura glared at her brother. 'That's what I said! What do you hate, Tomflynn?'

'Cold feet, I suppose. And biting flies. What about you, Donal?'

'I hate the *Sasanach*.'

'Why?'

'Because they hate us.'

Tom spent the day with Donal and his family. The two boys were sent to cut reeds for mending a section of damaged thatch on one of the cabins. Tom discovered that all reeds are not the same. Young green ones were useless for thatching, as were those that had died and gone brown and brittle. 'Reeds have to be mature but have plenty of life left in them,' Donal explained, 'because they must last for a long time.'

When that task was completed Bríd brought out a large sack of dried furze. She showed Tom how to cut and fold the spiky plants into neat, flat parcels called faggots. 'We use them for fuel in the bake-oven,' she explained. 'The outer edges blaze up quickly to warm the inside surface of the oven. The heart of the faggots burns with a deep, steady heat which is perfect for baking.'

'My father claims furze is useless,' Tom said.

'Nothing fashioned by God's hand is useless, Tomás. Furze also makes good fodder for horses. You chop up the green tops and pound them on a flat surface with a mallet. A horse fed with green furze will stay more fit than a horse given dry straw.'

While the bread was baking Seán showed Tom how to shape soft leather footgear from untanned deerskin. The old woman taught him the words of an ancient Gaelic lament. Donal's mother let him scale fish for the cooking pot. He tore the flesh badly at first, but Bríd just said, 'Try again.'

Everything he learned was a gift. Neither work nor play, but a treasure he could keep. It was great to feel useful for a change. He was having a wonderful time – except when he found himself imagining his father on a ship. And the pirates coming.

As the evening approached he knew he must go home. But first he asked Muiris, 'What do pirates do to the people on ships they capture?'

'They usually let them go after they surrender their valuables.'

'Usually?'

'Not always. Why do you ask?'

'My father is sailing to Dublin. He left yesterday morning.'

The skin tightened around the man's eyes. 'I see. When will he return?'

'He never tells us. He has business there, that's all I know. But about the pirates ... are there any pirates on the way to Dublin?'

The smile was in Muiris's eyes again. The smile which did

not reach his lips. 'There are always pirates, on land and sea. Is your father armed?'

'I don't know. He took some baggage with him, there might be weapons inside.'

Muiris said, 'If his ship is boarded by pirates he should be safe enough. Unless he resists.'

Tom's mouth went dry. 'He would never give up his valuables without a fight.'

'Then pray God, Tomás, your father never meets any pirates.'

• • • • • • •

CHAPTER TEN

ROWING

After Tom left, Donal set to work weaving a willow basket. His father needed some new lobster pots, but the boy had not yet mastered the complicated design. Baskets were good practice.

Yet even weaving a basket presented a problem this evening. All of Donal's fingers seemed to have turned into thumbs. His concentration was elsewhere.

His parents were talking about Tom Flynn.

No conversation in a cabin could be totally private. People who lived in cabins were expected to ignore anything not meant for them. Donal had grown up observing that ancient law. Tonight he broke it. He listened with all his might to the conversation between his parents.

His father was praising the other boy's courage. As far as Donal could tell, Tom had done nothing brave. He had sat in a boat. He had helped load and unload cargo. Nothing special, nothing manly. Nothing Donal could not have done himself, if his father gave him the chance.

Muiris said, 'The first time the lad was ever on open water, and he not seasick. He was born to it.'

I was born to it, Donal thought sourly. Tomás was born to the land.

He did not want to resent Tom; he liked Tom. They were good friends. But did his father have to praise the other boy so much? Muiris never praised his own son, at least not within Donal's hearing.

Donal stared down at the basket he was weaving. He had soaked the strips of willow in salt water to soften them, and waited until they were just pliable enough to force into shape without losing their springiness. He had done it so often the task was second nature to him. He did not even have to think about it, his hands knew what to do by themselves. Everything in the cabin, and the cabin itself, had been made by his family.

Tom Flynn said there were China plates in his house. And silver spoons, and glass bottles. He did not have to hunt and fish to feed himself nor gather firewood to keep himself warm. He had different suits of clothes in different colours, and some stockings of silk and others of wool, and more than one pair of shoes. With silver buckles on them.

Setting the basket aside, Donal lifted one of his feet and turned it over in his hands. He examined the thickly calloused sole. The leather soles of Tom's buckled shoes were thicker. No sharp bit of broken seashell could stab through them and leave a boy's foot bleeding and sore.

Tom Flynn had a fireplace in his bed-chamber. A fire-place with a hearth he did not have to share with anyone. He could sit there and soak up all the warmth himself. And he had a large bowl he called a 'chamber pot' that he could make water in during the night so he did not have to go out into the weather.

Donal wondered if any of the Flynn women lay awake all night coughing.

He put his foot down again and picked up the basket. He could smell rain on the wind. Summer would be over soon.

* * *

'Summer will be over soon,' Caroline Flynn reminded her mother. 'When is Father coming home?'

Catherine Flynn looked up from the sewing in her lap. 'I shall not know until he sends me a letter.'

'You should have had one by now,' Virginia said testily. 'Has Simon called to the village to see if the coach has come down from Dublin?'

'He has called several times. There is never any post from your father.'

'Perhaps he is sending it another way, then. An uncommon number of riders are passing by on the road. One of them may bring his letter.'

'A number of riders, dear?' Mrs Flynn tried to hide the sudden anxiety she felt. 'Why have you been going out to the road?'

'I like to watch people passing by. I try to guess where they are going and what will happen to them when they get there. Some of them will see towns and cities and go on ships and–'

'Enough, enough!' her mother exclaimed with a nervous laugh. 'Come sit here by me, both of you. We can work on your sister's trousseau together.'

Caroline looked at the pile of sewing with distaste. She loved to wear pretty clothes but did not like to make them. 'Why bother now?' she asked her mother. 'Wait until Father returns from Dublin. No doubt he will bring bales of beautiful fabric for her frocks.'

Mrs Flynn shook her head. 'I do not think so, not this time.'

'Of course he will,' Caroline contradicted. 'Father has bags of money and he loves to spend it on us. I can hardly wait to see what he brings us this time.' With her head full of silks and satins, William Flynn's youngest daughter flitted from the room.

She moves as lightly as a sunbeam, her mother thought to herself. I used to move like that once.

* * *

The second time Tom joined the smugglers was very different from the first. It started out much the same, with the pin-
prick of light sending its welcome signal, and the eager run
to the cliffs. Séamus was waiting as before. This time he was
not alone. He was in a large currach with two other men.
One of these was Fergal. The other was a brawny fellow Tom
had never met, but who had the familiar sea eagle features.
He held aloft a small lantern that was burning pilchard oil.
This was a by-product of pressing pilchards for salting, and
though it burned well the oil gave off a dreadful smell. No
pilchard oil was ever used at Roaringwater House.

'So this is the lad,' the man said to Séamus. His English,
Tom noted, was quite good.

'This is the lad,' Séamus agreed.

The man lifted the lantern higher so he could study Tom's
face. 'Are you old enough to do a man's work?'

Tom said in his deepest voice – which was not as deep as
he wanted – 'I can do anything you ask of me.'

He expected laughter at this boast. The man merely said,
'You will need that courage soon, and all the strength you
have.' He turned towards Séamus. 'It is a worry to me that
your brother agreed to this job tonight. There is a wee sliver
of moon tonight. And I have seen the sun dogs.'

Séamus replied in Irish. The lantern-holder grunted in
response.

'What are you talking about?' asked Tom.

'The weather,' Fergal said casually. Too casually. 'Into the boat with you, Tomás. We have a fair bit of rowing to do before this night's out.'

As he climbed into the boat Tom noticed there was an extra pair of oars. 'Am I going to row?' he asked eagerly.

'You are more than ballast on this night,' Séamus told him. 'Take up those oars and sit in the front. Watch me now. Hold them just as I do. Look at me, Tomás. Hold your oars like this.'

The man with the lantern lifted it high until Tom was settled, then extinguished the light.

They shoved off.

The oar handles had been worn smooth by many hands over the years. They felt just the way Tom had imagined they would. He listened intently as Séamus gave him instructions. 'The two oars must work as one, Tomás. Never let one go off by itself. The oars and your arms and your shoulders, all one.' At first the boy did not dig into the water enough. Then he went too deep. The other men tempered their own efforts until he had the feel of it. Biting his lip with concentration, soon Tom Flynn began to row in earnest. Began to become part of the rhythm.

Within moments they left the shore behind. Tom felt the bay heave under him like a living creature. He was not the least bit frightened now. I belong here, he thought, remembering that Donal had spoken those same words in the cave.

At first rowing was easy enough, even fun. Soon the effort became uncomfortable. Tom had never appreciated the difficulties of rowing before. The others made it look easy. His arms and shoulders flamed with pain. He gritted his teeth and ignored the discomfort. But he could not ignore the mighty force which was the bay. As if it had a will of its own, the water seemed determined to tear the oars from his hands.

He refused to give in. Head down, eyes clenched shut in agony, the boy continued to row.

Thud, swish, thud, swish, and the hiss of the waves. Time itself stopped. There was only darkness and pain and effort. It would last forever. This was Hell and he was in it.

'What o'clock is it?' the desperate boy asked.

No one answered. He tried again.

Séamus said, 'Look up.'

Puzzled but obedient, Tom opened his eyes. The stars had come out. So many stars! More stars than grains of sand on the beach; they jostled one another aside in the effort to share their glittering glory with Roaringwater Bay.

'The stars tell us all we need to know about where and when,' said Fergal.

'But ... how?'

The man with the lantern laughed. 'Learn, boy,' he said. 'Observe and learn.'

Thud, swish, thud, swish. The ache in Tom's muscles grew steadily worse. Then, 'Mind yourself, Tomás!' Séamus barked.

'There are submerged rocks here.'

'I don't see any.'

'You will see them right enough if we tear the boat open on one,' Séamus replied sternly. 'Row slowly now, keep the rhythm but feel down as you go, down with the oars until ...'

'Here,' said one of the other men.

'Raise your oars, Tomás. Quickly.'

Tom did as he was told. The man who had reported the submerged rock prodded the water with an oar, then pushed hard against something. The boat glided away from the unseen but deadly obstacle.

'How did you know a rock was there if you couldn't see it?' Tom wondered.

Fergal said, 'You cannot see your elbow, so how do you know it is there?'

The boy had no answer. Instead he devoted himself to his rowing.

Thud, swish, thud, swish.

And eventually it was a little easier.

Tom still had only a hazy notion of the geography of the bay, but he knew they were well beyond the river mouth when Séamus gave the order to rest their oars. The boy breathed a silent prayer of thanks. His muscles were trembling with fatigue and his back felt broken.

The crescent moon shed no light. The blaze of stars alone was enough to reveal a tiny island just ahead; it was little more than a tree-covered rock rising above the surface of the bay. Tom heard the familiar music of the oars as another currach detached itself from the shadows and came towards them.

Séamus called out, 'Are you ready?'

'We are ready,' Muiris called back to him.

In the second currach were Muiris and four other men, including Seán. The two boats lightly bumped each other. 'Take my place,' Muiris said to Séamus.

'I still think we should have brought a timber boat tonight,' Séamus replied. 'The sea is rough and we may have a heavy cargo.'

'The decision was mine to make,' Muiris reminded him.

Tom noticed that he spoke with calm authority. The voice of command.

Séamus quickly changed places with him.

'We need boats agile enough to move fast and keep us out of trouble,' Muiris explained as he settled himself beside Tom. 'Is your father still away?'

'He is still away.'

'Are you feeling strong this night, Tomás?'

'I am feeling strong,' Tom insisted. Knowing it was not true.

Muiris laughed. 'Glad I am to hear it, but save a bit for the work ahead. Give me the oars and rest yourself.' Muiris took Tom's place and said something in Irish to the other men.

The currach leaped forward like an eager horse at the touch of the spur.

Tom tilted his head back so he could gaze up at the stars. He had never seen anything so beautiful. An immense glittering tapestry stretching from here to forever. Was there a boat that could sail to forever?

'Ahead of us is Dún na Séad,' Muiris remarked after a time.

'The Fort of the Jewels,' Tom responded. 'The English call it Cape Clear island.'

'Well done, lad.'

'Are we going ashore there?'

'Not tonight. We will row past the southwest point of the island, where a rocky headland juts out into the sea. Atop this promontory is a half-destroyed castle. We are not going to land there, not this time, but watch for the place as we pass by. It is quite famous. Perhaps you have heard of it?'

Tom searched his memory. 'Never in my life,' he said.

'Are you certain?'

'I am certain.'

'That is a pity – though perhaps not a surprise,' Muiris said mysteriously. 'We have some time before we put you to work again, Tomás. Would you like to hear the story of Sir Fineen Ó Driscoll and the Castle of Gold?'

'Yes please!' said the boy.

CHAPTER ELEVEN
• • • • • • • • • •

THE CASTLE OF GOLD

'Clann Ó Driscoll takes its name from a king called Eidersceoil,' Muiris began. He fitted his words into the rhythm of the rowing, so they became one with the boat. And the night, and the sea. 'Eidersceoil ruled a vast portion of Munster in the tenth century. He was a direct descendant of Lugaidh Laidhe, founder of the Corca Laoidhe, for whom Cork is named.'

Tom wondered how these people who were long dead could have anything to do with him.

'The Castle of Gold, Dún an Óir, was built early in the thirteenth century,' Muiris continued. 'It stood a full three storeys high. From its heights one could see a great stretch of the coast, or look across five miles of Roaringwater Bay to Mount Gabriel and beyond.

'In the sixteenth century the castle was a favourite stronghold of the Ó Driscolls. Theirs was an ancient and honourable name, and the clan was prosperous. Their territory stretched from Kinsale to Kenmare. In 1573 the clan elected a new chieftain, Fineen Ó Driscoll. In accordance with Gaelic law, he took an oath to protect the territory belonging to his clan.

'Fineen's ancestors had been kings on this island since before the before, all through the Viking years and after the victory of Brian Boru. Then came an invasion the Irish could not repel. Led by a man called Strongbow, the invaders were of Norman blood and Catholic faith. In the name of an English king they occupied a number of Irish territories. Because they shared our faith, many of them adopted our language and customs. In time we learned to accommodate one another. We call them the Old English now, though in truth they have become almost as Irish as ourselves.

'As the years passed, a king of England turned his back on Rome and took up a new religion. When his daughter Elizabeth became queen she sent fresh armies to try to conquer Ireland. Soon the *Sasanach* were swarming over this country like a plague of rats. Seizing, looting, killing. Slaughtering women and children, turning rich land into scorched earth. They had an enormous appetite for destruction. We learned to hate these New English with all our hearts and we fought them with all our strength. We still fight them, Tomás. We will always fight them,' Muiris added in a low, sinister voice.

His tone sent a chill up Tom's spine. Suddenly the boy was interested.

'During those years Fineen Ó Driscoll had become the

most feared pirate in Ireland,' Muiris continued. 'Fineen the Rover, they called him. From his stronghold in Roaring-water Bay he and his followers boarded Spanish galleons and Dutch merchantmen and every English ship that sailed along the southern coast. The treasure they took came back to the Gael.'

Tom wondered if Fineen's followers were still out there. They might have boarded the ship his father was on! They might even have ...

Muiris interrupted his wild imaginings. 'Fineen was a cunning man, Tomás. When the English began fitting out larger warships to hunt him down, he took off his coat and turned it to the other side. He made friends with the *Sasanach*.'

Tom was shocked. 'That's awful!'

'Fineen would say it was just a matter of survival,' Muiris countered. 'He was good at survival. He convinced the English that he was their friend, whilst making the Irish believe he was still one of their own. They only began to have doubts when he went to London to meet Queen Elizabeth. She was known to have a *grá* for pirates.

'To everyone's surprise, in London Fineen traded his Gaelic title for an English knighthood. He also surrendered the territory remaining to his clan – which was not his personal property to give away. As reward for this treachery a portion of the land was re-granted to him. So was a new title. He returned to Roaringwater Bay as Sir Fineen Ó Driscoll.

'A man cannot take two sides and be true to them both, Tomás. In the end Ó Driscoll turned everyone against him. His clan splintered, with different factions going different ways. And the English, knowing what he was, never trusted him.

'After the battle of Kinsale English troops occupied Cape Clear and installed English settlers in the village of Baltimore. They mounted cannons on the high ground and blasted Dún an Óir to ruins. What remains is only a shell. Local people believe it is haunted. They never go there.'

The two boats rowed on together like a pair of horses in harness. Approaching the dark bulk of Cape Clear island, they began to follow its shoreline. The wind was rising. A heavy bank of cloud obscured the helpful stars. Try as he might, Tom could make out few details of the island. The boats rowed along its length for some three miles, until they came to a rugged headland.

At that moment the wind shifted. Briefly, the clouds lifted, as if swept aside by magic.

'Look up, Tomás!' Muiris commanded.

Tom looked up. Up a stark wall of rock, rising sheer from the roiling waves. Higher still, at the very top and eerily lit by starlight, he saw the tumbled towers and broken battlements of the Castle of Gold.

Tom's mouth went dry. 'Is it ... I mean, can it be ...' He licked his lips and tried again. 'Is it really haunted?'

No one answered. They rowed on.

Still spellbound by the ruined castle, at first Tom did not notice the increasing violence of the sea. As the waves mounted, a powerful current seized the two boats and tried to spin them off course. The oarsmen had to use all their skill to maintain control.

'Nothing to worry about,' Fergal assured the boy. 'It's always like this between here and the Fastnet.'

'What's the Fastnet?'

Muiris said, 'Fastnet Rock, Tomás. The sea here is more dangerous than anywhere else on the coast. Few ships will risk it, which suits our purpose. We want no witnesses to what we do tonight.'

The turbulence grew worse. The oarsmen grunted with effort. Tom was drenched by icy spray from the waves that battered the boat and a cold rain driven by a bitter wind. The rain slanted sideways, slamming into his face with the force of pebbles. He lost sight of the other currach.

'They'd better be here after all this,' Fergal muttered.

The voice of the gale rose to an inhuman howl.

The waves looked like mountains to Tom. The currach dropped into a deep valley, then rode up on a cresting wave only to plunge down again. The boy grabbed the side of the boat with both hands. He was too scared to be seasick. He longed to be back in Roaringwater House, with four stout walls around him and the weather locked outside.

Or did he? No matter what happened, would he not rather be here with Muiris and the others than anywhere else in the world?

A calm, strong voice reached him over the wind. 'Your first storm is always the worst, Tomás,' said Muiris.

Those words steadied the boy. He forced himself to take one hand from the side of the boat so he could wipe the water out of his eyes. He looked at the men hunched over their oars, obviously accustomed to rough seas. How brave they were! Tom wanted to be just like them.

They fought on. Then Tom heard a relieved cry, and a moment later he glimpsed a large ship through the rain. 'God bless the man,' Muiris said clearly.

Under his direction the currach was manoeuvred into the lee of the ship, where it could be partly shielded from the storm. The other currach soon joined them. A rope ladder was lowered down the side of the ship but the pounding sea made it dangerous to climb. Muiris would not let anyone else go with him. He had a brief, hard exchange about this with Séamus, but in the end Muiris won out.

Tom held his breath as he watched Muiris lean out of the currach to catch the swaying rope ladder, then go up hand over hand. There was a moment of relief when he safely made it over the rail and onto the deck. Then came a long wait, while the men at the oars struggled to maintain their position.

116

'Why don't we fasten our boats to the bottom of the ladder?' Tom asked Fergal.

'Because the wind could change at any time. We could be swept away by the sea and tear the ladder down with us. Worse still, we might be slammed against the side of the ship and have no way to escape before the currachs were crushed. Freedom is everything, Tomás.'

They continued to wait. Buffeted by the storm, swinging in a wild sea.

'Has something gone wrong?' Tom wanted to know.

Fergal said, 'You never know.' He sounded tense.

'Muiris told me this was safe.'

'Did he now?' Fergal gave an odd laugh, somewhere between a snort and a cough. 'Our friend has a strange idea of "safe".'

They waited. A man in the other currach began to whistle through his teeth. He was interrupted by a familiar shout from the deck. A loaded cargo net was lowered over the side. It struck the bottom of Tom's currach with a mighty thud. Two men swiftly removed a number of soft leather bags from the net. They placed the bags in the centre of the currach while the rest of the crew struggled to hold the vessel steady.

Surprisingly, when the net was only half empty it was hauled up again. Not taken back aboard ship, but left dangling against the side. Muiris called down a command in Irish to his men. The currach in which Tom rode moved

117

away to allow the other to take its place. The net was lowered once more. The remainder of its contents – more leather bags – were offloaded into the second currach.

'Why not put all the cargo in one boat?' Tom wondered aloud.

Fergal said, 'For safety's sake. With two boats, at least one should get back safely. To lose half of our load would be disaster enough, but to lose everything would be a catastrophe.' He untied the neck of one of the leather bags. 'Put your hand in there, Tomás. Do you feel something cold and hard? That is gold, lad. Solid gold.'

CHAPTER TWELVE

BURIED TREASURE

As soon as Muiris was safely back in the currach the boats rowed away. 'We are racing the light,' Muiris reminded his crew. 'If dawn catches us on open water some fisherman is bound to see us.'

A pale glow was visible in the east as they approached a tiny, tree-covered island. It might have been the one where they met Muiris earlier, Tom could not tell. The men rowed into the shallows and then just sat, looking at one another. Within moments the second currach joined them.

Fergal gave a great shout. 'We've done it!' he exulted. 'By all the saints and sinners, we've taken the Great Earl's gold!'

Seán said angrily, 'This is *not* the Great Earl's gold. Everything Richard Boyle has was stolen from the Irish, one way or another. We have just reclaimed a portion of it.'

'We have work to do,' Muiris reminded them.

They beached the currachs and unloaded the leather bags. The bags contained solid bars of pure gold. 'These are called ingots,' Muiris told Tom. They carried the bags to the centre

119

of the island, where a number of holes had been dug in advance. The gold ingots were deposited in the holes, which were then filled with earth. Finally their location was disguised by the natural debris of a woodland. Muiris was not satisfied until the scene appeared completely undisturbed.

By the time the task was finished, it was morning. Tom was exhausted. He had more questions than ever, but was too tired to ask them. It was all he could do to climb back into a currach. Muiris himself rowed the boy to the cove. The sun was climbing into a sky swept clean by the night's storm. 'You were a great help to us tonight, Tomás,' Muiris said as Tom got out of the boat. 'We needed speed and agility and you had both. Now ... can you get to your house without being seen?'

Tom managed a tired smile. 'I've had enough practice. But tell me, what will you do with the gold?'

Muiris looked tired too, there were dark circles under his eyes. 'I wondered how long it would take you to ask. The Earl of Cork has been moving large amounts of wealth around by sea to avoid the tax man. Those ingots probably were melted down from coins, jewellery, even gold plate. I rather doubt if the earl will make his loss public. It is in Richard Boyle's interest to keep the whole thing quiet.

'The captain of the ship will claim he was boarded by pirates. No one will find the culprits because no one will look very hard. When the time is right, we will remove the gold bars from the island and exchange them for coins that cannot be identified. There is a man in Limerick town who makes his living from such transactions. The ship's captain will receive a goodly share and a portion for his crew. If we are careful with it, the rest of the treasure will provide enough security for our sept and our children's children.' Muiris gave a satisfied sigh. 'Now, it's home for you, lad. While your father is away you are the man of the family. Tonight you have proved you are up to the task.'

* * *

The storm had heralded the change of seasons. Soon the wind from the bay dripped autumn over the land. One storm followed another, until Tom could barely recall the radiant days of summer.

In September Tom's tutor arrived at Roaringwater House. Nicholas Beasley had long thin arms and short spindly legs, a bald head he disguised with a cheap wig, and a bulging Adam's apple that bobbed up and down when he spoke. He rode a swaybacked brown mare who looked older than he was. His canvas saddlebags were stuffed to bursting with books, notebooks, maps, charts, inks, pens, chalk, and a greying blackboard.

In previous years Tom had been glad to see him. Behind Beasley's unimpressive face was a brain packed with fascinating facts. If Tom showed interest in a particular subject, his tutor could pour out knowledge like cream from a pitcher.

This year was different. Lessons made an unwanted claim on Tom's time. He had to put away his magic pony. No more visits to the bay. No more swimming. No more happy days with his friends in the narrow valley. Combined with the onset of bad weather, Mr Beasley's appearance made Tom a virtual prisoner in Roaringwater House.

When Herbert Fox paid a call on Elizabeth it was obvious the engagement was not going well. Even the servants commented on it. The couple had little to say to each other. Fox showed more interest in Flynn's wine cellar than in his daughter. Elizabeth spent most of the time in her chamber. When they sat at table together she only picked at her food.

Fox confirmed that William Flynn had booked passage on one of his ships. 'We spoke together before he departed,' the man told Mrs Flynn, 'and from the ship's captain I know he arrived safely. I have no idea where he went or what he did after that. His movements have nothing to do with me. Nothing at all,' Fox stressed.

He left Roaringwater House after only two days. Elizabeth's spirits improved at once.

Mrs Flynn waited anxiously for a letter, or even a short note, but none came. She did not say anything about it to the children, she did not want to worry them, but she was increasingly withdrawn.

Only Caroline noticed. One morning she intercepted Tom in the passageway. 'I'm afraid Mother is ill,' she said.

'She's never very well,' he pointed out.

'I know, but this is different. I tried to show her one of my gloves that had split a seam. Mother will talk about clothes no matter how poorly she feels. Yet this time she wouldn't even answer me. And she had such an expression in her eyes ... I can't describe it, but something is wrong, Tom. Really, truly wrong.'

'Did you tell Lizzie or Ginny?'

'I tried but they won't listen to me. I'm just "giddy, silly Caro" to them. I may be giddy but I'm not stupid. I notice things.' As she spoke, Caroline was looking closely at her brother. He had grown during the summer. He was taller and leaner, with colour in his face. 'Will you talk to Mother, Tom?'

'I'll try,' he said.

But Mrs Flynn had no intention of discussing her problems with her little boy, her last baby. She called him impertinent. 'Really, Tom, I do not know what has got into you. I must ask Mr Beasley to teach you some respect.'

'I agree with you, Caro,' Tom told his sister afterwards. 'Either Mother is ill, or she has a serious problem, but she won't tell me.'

'Then what can we do?'

Tom squared his shoulders. 'I'll think of something,' he

promised. He had no idea what that might be, though saying the words made him feel better. As if he really could do it.

* * *

'Why doesn't Tomflynn come to see us any more?' Maura asked Donal.

He looked up from the rope he was plaiting. 'I don't know. Maybe he likes that big house of his better than he likes us.'

The answer did not satisfy Maura. She went to her mother. 'Does Tomflynn hate me?'

'Light of my heart, who could hate you?' the woman said with a laugh. She swept Maura into her arms and gave her a big hug.

That was no answer either. Maura went where she always went when she needed to think. She crawled under one of the overturned currachs. For the first time in many days the sun was shining. Its heat warmed the leather shell of the boat, comforting the little girl inside.

Tomflynn could not like his house better than he likes me, she told herself. Could he? I like him better than I like my house.

Something else must be wrong. I had best go see.

She crawled out from under the currach and set out to find Tom.

* * *

The first sunshine in ages, Tom thought glumly. And I'm trapped here.

'Here' was the former nursery at Roaringwater House, fitted out as a schoolroom. At the front of the room Mr Beasley was droning on and on about the twelve Caesars – or was it ten? – it did not matter anyway. They were all dead.

With his forefinger, Tom flicked a dead fly off the table that served as his desk. He yawned. It was late afternoon, the time of day when boys are inclined to grow sleepy over their schoolbooks. Dust motes danced in the shaft of sunlight from the nearest window. Drying ink at the mouth of Tom's inkpot took on the colours of the rainbow.

Rainbows over the bay.

'Thomas!' Mr Beasley said abruptly. 'Are you paying attention?'

'I am, sir.'

'Then perhaps you would humour me by naming the exports of Ireland to Spain and Portugal. Stand up, please.'

'Spain and Portugal?' Tom queried, playing for time.

Beasley nodded.

'The exports are ... er ...' Tom's brain was racing. He cleared his throat and began again. 'Pilchards, cod, hake, salmon skins for gloves, beans, iron, linen ...' he rolled his eyes and looked at the ceiling, '... pipe-staves, butter and tallow. Sir.' He heaved a sigh of relief and sat down.

There was a knock at the door. Mr Beasley scowled at the

interruption. A moment later Virginia thrust her head into the room. 'Tom? There is the funniest little girl downstairs, asking for you.'

But she was no longer downstairs. She pushed past Virginia and ran straight to Tom. 'I'm not funyest and I'm not little!' she cried, stamping her feet in indignation. 'Tell her, Tomflynn.'

'Maura! What brings you here?'

The child noticed Mr Beasley staring at her bare toes. 'Your eye is crookit,' she told him. 'Does it hurt much?' Before the astonished tutor could respond she said, 'I'm Tomflynn's friend, Maura. I want to know if he likes this house better'n me.'

'I like you and your family better than anybody,' Tom assured her.

Maura rewarded him with a dazzling smile. Virginia was frowning. 'What are you talking about?' she asked her brother. 'Just who is this person, Tom? And what is her family to you?'

'She told you; they're my friends.'

'I see,' said Virginia, who did not see at all. She bent down until her face was level with Maura's. 'I should like to be your friend too.' She spoke in the too-sweet voice adults commonly use for infants.

Maura regarded her solemnly, then held up two small hands with fingers spread wide. 'I have this many friends now,' she informed Virginia. 'Can't have more 'til I have more fingers.'

Tom burst into laughter. 'Did you come all the way here by yourself, Maura, or did Donal bring you?'

Her eyes danced. 'By myself!'

Tom glanced towards his tutor. 'A gentleman would walk you home, is that not right, Mr Beasley?' He extended a hand to the child, who took it with perfect trust. 'Come now, Maura, the hour is late and we'd best be going.' Without waiting for permission from anyone, he led her from the room.

Halfway down the front stairs they met Mrs Flynn coming up. When she saw Maura one hand flew to her throat. The other hand gripped the banister until the knuckles were white. 'Where did you come from?' she gasped.

• • • • • • • • •

CHApter thirteen

MR FLYNN MAKES A FRIEND

there must be many paths by now, thought William Flynn. Paths not visible to the naked eye, yet worn as surely as chariot tracks in the stony roads of Rome. Paths marking my pilgrimages to the doors of the great and grand. Once they were happy enough to see me. Now that I need them, none of them want to know me.

So I drag myself back to Dublin Castle one more time. The Castle swarms with administrators and lawyers and clerks and accountants and hangers-on. I want to be a hanger-on, just give me something to hang on to! Instead I sit and wait. And wait. Until I am told to return the following day. Or the day after that. Or next week. Or perhaps after the first of the month?

Flynn had long since swallowed what was left of his pride, and made a direct appeal to his companions at the coffee house. 'You have connections, all of you. We have done business together, surely that means something! All I need is to get my name on the right list.'

His coffee house friends knew that in difficult times a man must guard his assets. They offered Flynn sympathy but kept their connections to themselves.

He knew he should write a reassuring letter to his wife to keep her spirits up. But he could not bring himself to put pen to paper. He knew only too well that she valued truth above all other virtues.

Every day he asked at the post office, hoping for a letter from her. But there never was one. Either she was too ill to write – though in that case surely Virginia would have written – or there was no disaster at home. Yet.

Meanwhile his funds were dwindling. His major source of income was gone. He could not ask his wife for money from the supply he had left for running the household. She must never know that they were hanging on by their fingertips!

He moved from a fashionable inn to a simple lodging house. His diet changed from flesh meats and French brandy to boiled eels and beer. William Flynn, who once set the finest table in West Cork.

In the crooked laneways and foul gutters of Dublin he saw what could become of Irish Catholics who had no property.

He no longer frequented the coffee house. He could not bear to be pitied by men who once admired him. The end of every unsuccessful day found him wandering along the banks of the Liffey. The state of the river suited his mood. When the tide was out the Liffey stank of sewage and dead animals, in spite of the handsome buildings rising on either bank. Sometimes he wondered what would happen to him if he fell in the water. The filth probably would poison him before the river could drown him. William Flynn was careful not to get too close to the bank. He was a dreamer. *Something good will happen tomorrow*. He still believed that.

Just barely.

One misty evening he recognised a familiar figure on the New Bridge. The man was headed away from him, crossing to the opposite bank of the Liffey. Flynn shouted a name, but the wind snatched the word from his lips and blew it away.

Flynn ran towards the bridge as fast as he could.

As he ran an idea entered his head. There were only three bridges spanning the river: Old Bridge, New Bridge, and the infamous Bloody Bridge, scene of several riots. Surely that was not enough for a fast-growing capital city. Another bridge near the Custom House would make perfect sense.

If I were in the Dublin administration I would propose it, he told himself. *Perhaps they would even name it after me. The William Flynn Bridge. How noble it sounds. Catherine would be proud.*

If I want to be part of the Dublin administration I must catch up with that man ahead of me!

* * *

Maura's mother longed to scold her daughter, but she was unwilling to quench the child's bright spirit. 'A thousand thanks for bringing her back to us, Tomás,' Bríd said. 'I thought she was with Donal until he came in alone. He and Seán just went to look for her.'

'I was in Tomflynn's house!' Maura exclaimed. 'It's awful big but he likes me better, he said so. Did you not, Tomflynn?'

Tom nodded. 'I did indeed.'

'I frighted Tomflynn's mother, too!' the child went on.

'Surely not, dear heart. Who could be frightened of you?'

'Maura didn't frighten my mother,' Tom said, 'she merely startled her. Mother didn't expect to see a strange little girl in our house. I can explain to her when I go home – which I must do at once.'

'Och, Tomás, I will not hear of it. Stop with us for a while and have something to eat. Muiris and Séamus are away for a few days but the others will be that glad to see you. We feared you had forgotten us. Wait whilst I find Donal and Seán, they cannot be far ...'

Tom put up his hand. 'Please, I can't stay. The days are getting shorter. I don't want to go along the edge of the cliffs after dark.'

Leabharlanna Poibli Chathair Baile Átha Cliath
Dublin City Public Libraries

By the time Tom returned to Roaringwater House his mother had gone to bed. Virginia and Elizabeth were waiting for him. 'How dare you upset Mother so!' an angry Virginia challenged. 'She is quite ill tonight. What possessed you to bring a strange child into this house? And why did you leave so hastily without any explanation?'

He did not want to tell the whole story to his sisters. He did not even want to tell it to his mother. On the way home he had been thinking of the best way to give her a partial account without revealing his involvement with the smugglers.

'The little girl's name is Maura,' he said. 'Her brother and I play together.'

'Do you ride to meet him on your hobby-horse?' Elizabeth teased.

'Only sometimes; other times I walk. It's quite a journey for a small girl, though. We hurried away this afternoon so she would be safe at home before dark.'

Tom's sisters exchanged glances. He was not sure if they believed him, but they did not know the right questions to ask.

At last Elizabeth said, 'I suppose you do get lonely. We all get lonely, Tom.'

* * *

William Flynn hurried across the timber bridge. The other man had already reached the bank and was putting the river behind him. The distance between them was growing fast.

Flynn gave one last despairing shout.

The figure he was pursuing paused, stopped. Turned around. Waited until Flynn came running up to him, panting. Only then did Flynn realise his mistake. Seen from a distance the stranger could easily be mistaken for the Earl of Cork. He had the same sloping shoulders and hurried walk. But this was neither Richard Boyle nor his son Roger. Dressed in a suit and cloak of black velvet, he was a youth of no more than fourteen or fifteen. He had a large frame and a long, horsy face. 'Do I know you, sir?' he asked in an educated English accent.

'Apparently not,' said Flynn. 'I thought I knew you, but—'

'I fear you took me for my father. Allow me to introduce myself. My name is Robert Boyle. I have been studying at Eton for the past four years.'

William Flynn introduced himself and sought to start a conversation. He was not used to talking with boys. 'I have a son who is almost your age,' he began.

'Are the two of you close?'

The question surprised Flynn. Obviously, this was important. 'Close? Ah ... yes, yes, of course we are. I positively dote on the lad. We have the most wonderful times together.'

'Your son is a fortunate fellow,' said Robert Boyle. 'I should like to meet him. Sadly, my time in Ireland is over for now. Tomorrow I sail to the Continent to study French and Italian, as well as the work of the great stargazer, Galileo. You know of him, of course?'

'Of course,' murmured Flynn – who had never heard of Galileo. 'We must make the most of the time available to us. Have you dined yet?' As he spoke he was trying to remember how much he had in his purse. Was there enough to pay for an impressive meal?

'Thank you,' young Boyle replied, 'but we had supper before I came out for my walk.' Good manners prompted him to add, 'Perhaps, Mr Flynn, you would be so kind as to take breakfast with us in the morning?'

With us. With the Earl of Cork and his son! William Flynn could hardly believe his good fortune.

He could not sleep and arose early. To his dismay, he realised his best coat looked shabby. The lace on his cuffs was limp. His white cravat was spotted with food stains. His favourite cambric shirt had dark sweat stains in the armpits and smelled like a dogfight. There was no time to have new clothes made, even if he could spare the money. He did what he could to improve his appearance, then went to meet his hosts for breakfast, at the same fashionable inn where Flynn himself once stayed.

This morning young Boyle was wearing dark green. His lace cuffs and ivory silk cravat were immaculate. He had only one companion, a Frenchman whom he introduced as his tutor. Noticing Flynn's disappointment, the lad said, 'Were you expecting my father to join us?'

'I hoped ...'

The sudden coldness in Boyle's voice was unmistakable. 'You will not meet the earl in my company. I spend as little time with him as possible.'

Flynn's brain hurried to catch up, as his body had done the night before. 'I hoped your father would not be here,' he claimed. 'I am not one of his admirers. My business in the capital is with Thomas Wentworth. I need to speak with him on a matter of some urgency, but for some reason his staff in Dublin Castle keep putting me off.'

'Did they not tell you? The Lord Deputy has been called to London as adviser to the king. Charles wants his help in quelling the Scottish uprising.'

London. Flynn's heart sank. While he was digesting this upsetting news, young Boyle added, 'Those who know believe that Thomas will be created Earl of Strafford as a reward for his services.'

'Good for him,' Flynn said faintly. 'You called the Lord Deputy Thomas. Are you a friend of his?'

'I would not say we are friends; he is an austere man who keeps himself to himself for the most part. But I have met him on occasion and I like him. We have something in common, Thomas and I.'

'Oh? What is that?'

'We both hate my father,' Boyle replied. 'Thomas detests

the earl for his politics, and I despise him for the way he makes his money.'

'I am in total agreement!' said William Flynn. 'How refreshing to meet such a frank young man.'

Breakfast was a pleasant meal. Roast meats and boiled eggs and, wonder of wonders, tea. The Frenchman ate little and said less, but drank quantities of tea. Flynn found it surprisingly easy to talk to Robert Boyle. Soon he was relating his unsuccessful attempts to gain the earl's support.

'I doubt if your problem can be charged to any prank by your son,' Boyle told him. 'My father has many faults, but he is not as petty as that. I suspect he is avoiding you because you are a Catholic.'

'How did you know that?'

The lad smiled. 'One can always tell,' he said. 'I myself would not hold it against you. Some of the best people I know are Catholics. My father feels differently. He would never give a Catholic a responsible position with the government. He is happy to eat their food or drink their wine, but that is as far as his tolerance extends.'

'I had hopes ...'

Young Boyle looked sympathetic. 'Hopes butter no bread,' he said gently.

By the time the meal was over Flynn felt that he had made a friend. It was a pity his new friend was only a lad and could do him no good.

As they rose to leave the table, Boyle reached into a pocket of his waistcoat and took out a small case made of eel-skin. He extracted an oblong of white pasteboard from the case and gave it to Flynn. 'Please hand in my calling card to the Lord Deputy's personal secretary,' he said.

Flynn glanced down at the card. 'I should not think the name of Boyle was popular in the offices of Thomas Wentworth.'

The youngster's eyes twinkled. 'My name is popular enough with Thomas Wentworth's secretary. The secretary's daughter and I are betrothed to marry three years hence, when I return from my studies on the Continent. For my sake I am certain he will help you. Or there is Robert Arthur, a Dublin alderman and Master of the Guild of Merchants. He is a Catholic like yourself and his son, Ignatius, is my best friend. Feel free to call on them in my name. They understand the difficulties of being a Catholic in the city.

'And by the by, do forgive your son his mischief. I envy him, having a father who dotes on him.'

* * *

Catherine Flynn stayed in her bed day after day. When any of her children looked in on her she always asked the same question: 'Is there any word from your father?' The answer was always the same. 'Not yet.'

Her response was to sigh and turn her face to the wall.

At first Tom was glad she did not ask him to explain about Maura. All her thoughts were of her husband now. She had been thin; she became skeletal. Several times a day one of the servants carried a tray up to her chamber, laden with delicacies to tempt her appetite. The tray was returned to the kitchen untouched.

On a raw morning when the wind gibbered and moaned around the chimneys, Simon was sent to Ballydehob to fetch a doctor. After a long wait the doctor arrived. He was a short, thickset man in a grey frieze overcoat. He did not wear a gentleman's cravat because he was not a gentleman. Like many doctors, he was also a barber. He carried the tools of his professions in a badly scuffed black bag.

He was shown to Mrs Flynn's chamber. Tom and his sisters followed. They watched in silence while he bent over the bed and studied her face. 'Your mother's blood is too thick,' he announced as he straightened up. 'It has congested her organs.'

Opening his black bag, the doctor took out a set of steel-bladed knives wrapped in flannel. He tested several of the blades with his thumb. When he was satisfied with their sharpness, he laid two of the knives side by side on Mrs Flynn's writing desk and put the rest back in the bag.

'You must leave the room now,' he informed his audience,

'whilst I give this poor woman some relief.'

Tom and his sisters waited anxiously outside the closed door. The servants gathered around them, listening as intently as they were. For a few minutes they heard nothing. Then Mrs Flynn gave a sharp cry.

I am the man of the family now, Tom reminded himself. He threw open the door and entered the chamber.

CHAPTER FOURTEEN

CHRISTMAS

Catherine Flynn looked dead. Her eyes were closed and sunken. Her breathing was so shallow it did not lift the blanket. One of her arms hung over the side of the bed. From a cut in her forearm a thin stream of blood dripped into a basin on the floor.

Tom was horrified. 'What have you done?' he cried. The doctor gaped at him. The boy reached out and seized the man by the front of his coat. 'What have you done to my mother, you maggot!'

The doctor tried to pull away, but Tom held on grimly.

'I bled her, of course,' the doctor said. 'Release me at once, sir.'

Tom had never been addressed as 'sir' before. He loosened his hold but did not release the doctor entirely. 'Mother was as pale as a sheet before you came. Now she's even whiter. You've made her worse.'

With an effort, the man freed himself from Tom's grasp. He said indignantly, 'I did no such thing. I was helping her,

140

you young fool. Your lady mother is suffering from the black melancholy. The humours of her body are foul and polluted. Bleeding is the standard remedy for such ailments.'

'No one with a head on his shoulders would believe such nonsense,' Tom angrily declared. 'There is nothing "foul and polluted" about my mother. Get out of this house before I throw you down the stairs!' At that moment he looked as if he could do it.

The doctor snatched up his bag and implements and scurried from the room. The three girls, crowded together at the doorway, moved aside to let him pass.

Tom beckoned to them. 'Help me here, Lizzie.' He pulled a handkerchief from his pocket to staunch the flow of blood. 'Caro, run and find clean linen for bandages. Ginny, fetch the brandy.'

They soon stopped the flow of blood and bound the arm. Then Tom and Elizabeth raised Mrs Flynn enough to allow Caroline to plump her pillows. Ginny tilted a spoon of brandy between her lips. After a few moments she opened her eyes. She looked from one face to another. 'What happened?' she whispered.

'It's over now,' Elizabeth said soothingly. 'Do not concern yourself.'

'It hurt more than I expected. When he cut into my arm ...'

'The filthy maggot,' growled Tom. 'He won't be allowed in this house ever again, I'll see to that.' His new confidence surprised everyone – most of all himself.

Slowly, Mrs Flynn began to recover. She tried not to worry so much about her husband. She saw that she had frightened the children, and she wanted to be strong for them.

Meanwhile Tom put Donal's family out of his mind. Most of the time. They were part of another life entirely. His life was in Roaringwater House now, where he was needed.

His lessons with Mr Beasley continued. When their day's work together was done, Tom took his books into his mother's chamber for study. It was pleasant to be there, knowing she was nearby. Sometimes he saw her watching him. They exchanged smiles.

She is getting well, he thought. It helps her to have me here.

He began asking the occasional question so she would think she was helping him.

One rainy afternoon Tom looked up from sharpening the nib of his quill. 'Mother? I don't suppose you know any Latin?'

'*Sic semper tyrannis*,' she said softly.

Tom put down his penknife. 'What was that?'

'*Sic semper tyrannis*. A phrase in Latin. It means "thus always to tyrants". Supposedly the slogan was shouted by the Roman senators who murdered Julius Caesar in the Forum.'

Tom was astonished. 'Where did you learn that?'

'In my family we all knew Latin. I have forgot most of it, I'm afraid.'

In my family. She had never mentioned her family before. As far as Tom knew, her life had begun with her marriage to William Flynn.

Why was I not curious? he asked himself. But now that he was curious she would not talk about it. When he asked, 'What were you mother and father like?' she said only, 'I hardly remember them any more.'

October became November and Mrs Flynn was up and about again. Still thin and pale, but stronger. She even joined Tom at the door to wave goodbye to his tutor when Mr Beasley left until the following spring.

A few days later, the long-awaited letter arrived. It was very brief.

My dearest Kate,

At last there is good news to report. Here in Dublin I have found unexpected allies, and now see a way to resolve our troubles. I regret that I must remain in the capital for a while longer. You may think I am taking a risk, staying away from Roaringwater at this time, but you must trust me. Be assured that everything will come right in the end. ...

Catherine Flynn read the letter twice. Then she folded the small sheet of paper and sat staring into the fire. When Tom entered the room she did not look up.

'Your father is not coming home,' she said over her shoulder.

143

Tom's immediate, frightened thought was of pirates. 'Was he kidnapped?'

His mother turned to stare at him. 'Of course not. Why ever did you say that?'

'I don't know. I mean ...' He scuffed the floor with his toe, feeling like a child again.

'Please do not worry, Tom,' she said, trying to sound as if there were nothing to worry about. 'William has sent good news. The Lord Deputy is in England with King Charles. In the new year Thomas Wentworth will receive an earldom. Then he plans to return to Ireland and raise an army to fight for the king in Scotland.'

'What has any of that to do with Father?'

'Your father is staying in Dublin until the Lord Deputy arrives. Thanks to friends in high places, William expects to be offered a commission in the new army. An officer's commission is highly prized; it comes with a number of privileges. William's appointment will give us security at last.'

Tom was puzzled. He had always taken his security for granted. 'What about this house, Mother, and our land? Are they not all the security we need?'

'Wait until your father comes home, Tom. He can explain much better than I can.'

Once again, Tom thought, I'm being treated like a child. But I'm not a child. There are places where I'm treated like a man.

After her husband's letter arrived Mrs Flynn's appetite improved. She spent less time in her bedchamber and more with her family. She and her daughters played card games or did their sewing together. Sometimes Elizabeth and Caroline sang English ballads in clear, sweet voices.

Tom rarely joined them. He took to wandering about the house, looking out of the windows.

'That boy is like a bird in a cage,' Elizabeth remarked. 'Whatever is wrong with him?'

'He misses his father,' her mother replied.

'He's growing up,' said Virginia.

Winter brought short dark days and long cold nights. A fire was lit in every fireplace, yet still Tom felt cold. Something was wrong. He knew it the way Bríd and Seán always knew when a storm was coming. It must involve his father. A terrible fate might have befallen him.

Tom began having nightmares that he could not quite remember afterwards. But he knew they were awful.

The entire household became involved in 'bringing in' the Christmas. Once again the servants scrubbed and polished the house from top to bottom. Virginia drew up a shopping list which included twenty pounds of beeswax, pure white and faintly smelling of honey. The wax was slowly melted in an iron cauldron. Tom measured and cut the lengths of wick while Elizabeth and the housekeeper dipped the candles.

A special large candle was lit on the first day of Advent.

The arrival of the Holy Season was marked by frost-coloured sky and frost-spangled earth. At night, if there were no clouds, a million stars glittered, hard and bright, like gifts of diamonds from the Magi. The wind from the bay smelt of ice. Two pigs were butchered, one for the family and one for the servants' table, and their blood was drained and set aside. Tom contributed more spices from his carefully hidden store, and Cook filled the house with the smell of boiling puddings.

The servants were sent to collect cartloads of holly and ivy. They left at dawn and returned at dusk, since neither plant grew near the bay. On the following day Catherine Flynn and her children were busy tying ribbon into bows and arranging wreaths and swags.

That night they lit candles in all the windows.

Mrs Flynn wanted to buy special treats for the Christmas table as well as the traditional New Year's presents for the family. Usually her husband took care of such things, but his prolonged absence left the task to her.

She asked Tom to accompany her to the village market at Skibbereen. It was the first time she had asked him to be her escort. He was proud of the honour, but concerned for his mother. 'Are you sure you feel strong enough?' he asked.

'I do feel strong enough, but it might be best if you drive the dogcart. Do you think you can handle the pony, Tom?'

He started to tell her he could handle the oars of a currach on the open sea, then thought better of it.

The grey pony had taken members of the Flynn house-hold to market for fifteen years. She knew the way better than any human. As soon as her passengers were settled in the wicker cart, she started off on her own at a steady trot. Tom flicked the whip above her haunches once or twice anyway. Her only response was to lay back her ears.

'Do not torment the animal,' said his mother.

As they neared the village, the road on either side blos-somed with stalls selling everything from local produce to imported luxuries. Stallholders called out to Mrs Flynn as she passed by. Tom said, 'They seem to know you, Mother.'

She arranged the hood of her cloak to hide more of her face. 'They do not know me,' she said.

Soon the road was crowded with people who went from stall to stall, examining the goods on offer. Shoppers loudly haggled with merchants. Small children ran madly about, shrieking at the top of their lungs. Cattle and sheep and poultry were all available for sale; the air was thick with the smell of them. Dogs barked, geese honked, an ass brayed – and the grey pony came to a halt.

'I shall wait with the cart,' said Mrs Flynn, pulling her hood even farther over her face. She gave Tom a shopping basket, a list and a small purse of coins.

Feeling wonderfully important, he tied the reins and stepped from the cart. As he crossed the road a boy on a shaggy plough horse galloped past. The animal's huge hooves threw up a spray of cold mud. Tom tried to wipe a gobbet of mud from his cheek, but only succeeded in smearing it.

He went from stall to stall looking for the things his mother wanted. It took a while to find them all. Wide red ribbon for tying up wreaths. Metal polish. A bottle of camphor to keep moths out of woollens, a packet of needles, a set of pudding bowls, a new shopping basket. Tom knew how to weave a basket. But he could not tell his mother without explaining where he had learned.

The last items on the list were the special treats the girls loved at Christmas. Several stalls offered them, but they were shockingly expensive and no one was buying. The small purse was nearly empty anyway. Tom headed back to the dogcart to ask his mother for more money.

The grey pony was standing where he left her, but the cart was empty.

Tom felt a flash of panic. If something happened to his mother while she was in his care, his father really would kill him!

Then he saw her coming towards him, her arms loaded with parcels. Relief washed over him. 'You gave me a fright, Mother. You should have warned me you would not stay with the cart.'

'I was buying presents for us to exchange at the New Year. Something for each of you and your father too, even though he won't be with us. Did you get everything on my list?'

'All except the sweetmeats. Raisins and figs and sugared almonds are very dear and I ran out of money. The woman at the stall said they cost twice as much this year as last, because they are imported. If you want I shall go back for them.'

Catherine Flynn shook her head. 'Perhaps we had best make do with what we have, Tom.'

She was quiet on the drive back to Roaringwater House, wondering why her husband had not sent additional money for the holidays. Wondering if everything really was all right. Wondering.

At the house, Caroline thrust out her lower lip. When she was sulky her beauty vanished. 'It just won't be Christmas without sugared almonds.'

'Christmas is not about treats, Caroline. It is about the birth of hope, which we need more,' said her mother.

'I hoped to have sugared almonds!'

On the day of Christ's birth a priest came to Roaringwater House to say Mass in the private chapel. Elizabeth and Caroline had decorated the little chapel with holly, while Virginia had contributed a watercolour painting of the Virgin and Child.

It seemed strange to Tom that his father was not with them. As he knelt to pray, Tom wondered how, and where, Muiris and his family celebrated Christmas. Suddenly he could see their faces as clearly as if they stood before him. And longed with all his heart to be with them. When he awoke on St Stephen's Day he could not wait any longer.

* * *

Mud and ice had made the ground dangerously slippery. Because it was the middle of winter Tom was not barefoot. He soon realised his mistake, and stopped to take off his shoes and stockings. He did not slip and slide as much when his toes could grip the earth, but soon his feet were so cold they felt numb. He had to put his shoes back on. If he were at home he could warm his feet on the fender.

His damp stockings began to chafe his muddy feet and make them sore. He could feel the blisters rising but he kept going. Why was the journey taking so long? Where were the familiar landmarks? Was it possible he had made a wrong turn?

Surely not. He knew the way, of course he did. Scramble up one more steep hill, wade through a sea of dead bracken, and ...

And there was the little river below him.

Below him? He should not have been overlooking the stream. He should have been walking along its bank. He started down.

The voice of the wind, always present in the bay, changed abruptly. A hiss of sleet warned Tom only moments before the storm hit.

CHAPTER FIFTEEN

A TERRIBLE ACCIDENT

Maura laughed.

She and her brother were sitting on three-legged stools beside the hearth. Firelight painted the walls of the cabin with a rosy glow. Donal was pulling faces to distract Maura from any possible rumble of thunder. The children were alone in the cabin while their parents paid a call upstream.

'Now I'm a brown hare,' said Donal. He lifted his upper lip. 'See what big teeth I have? See my long funny ears?' He waggled his fingers beside his head.

'Show me a deer, Don-don. A big red deer with lots of branches.'

'You mean antlers?'

The little girl held up one hand. 'Ssshhh.'

'I thought you wanted–'

'SSSHHH! I hear something.'

151

'Only the wind, and it won't hurt you,' Donal said.

She shook her head. 'Not the wind. Listen!'

To humour her, he cupped his hands behind his ears. And listened.

The wailing cry could have been anything. A sea bird flying over the marsh. Or even the bark of a seal.

The sound stopped, replaced by the cheerful crackle of the fire. Donal drew a breath to speak but Maura shook her head at him. 'Wait,' she said.

The cry came again.

'That's Tomflynn!' Maura exclaimed.

'It can't be.'

But she was already on her feet and running to the door.

They found him at the edge of the narrow valley, lying on his back, eyes closed, arms flung out, sleet beating against his face. His right leg was bent at an unnatural angle.

Maura flung herself onto the ground beside him. 'Tom-flynn, wake up!'

He opened his eyes and looked at her. 'I'm not asleep.' He sounded hoarse.

'We heard you calling for help,' Donal said. 'Did you fall down the hill?' He glanced up the steep slope. 'It's covered with ice, that.'

'I must have done, I don't remember. Everything went white. Or black. I don't remember,' he repeated.

Donal extended his hand. 'Here, let me help you.'

Tom tried to rise, then fell back with a gasp of pain. Maura scowled. 'Don't hurt him, can't you see he's busted?'

'I can see that. Run and get Seán and Séamus. Tell them what's after happening.'

'Run yourself,' the little girl retorted. 'Your legs are longer.' Lifting her skirt, she pulled down her flannel petticoat. She folded it to put beneath Tom's head. 'Run!' she shouted at her brother.

He ran.

As soon as Donal was out of earshot Maura told Tom, 'It was me heard you, Tomflynn.'

'I was afraid no one would.'

'I know your voice. I know the wind's voice. It was me heard you.'

Waves of agony swept along Tom's body like the waves of the sea. He tried to hold them back but they were stronger than he was. He clutched the little girl's hand. He knew he was squeezing too hard but he could not help it.

She bit her lip and let him squeeze.

Tom lost all sense of time. After a year at least, Seán and Séamus arrived with a litter made of blankets and two oars. The men laid the litter on the earth beside Tom and asked if he could roll onto it.

'I don't think so.' The boy's forehead was drenched with icy sweat.

Donal crouched down so Tom could see his face. 'Yes,

you can,' he said.

Donal sounded so much like Muiris that Tom believed him. One agonised effort and he was on the litter. The pain made him sick to his stomach.

The two men lifted the litter as carefully as possible. Before they had gone far one of the blankets slipped, and the whole thing had to be re-tied. They set off again. Donal walked on one side and Maura on the other. The last thing Tom was aware of was an open doorway. And the cheerful crackle of a fire.

'Wait for Bríd and Muiris,' Séamus told Seán. 'You do not know how to mend broken bones.'

His brother was offended. 'I am not trying to mend his bones. The lad is shivering and I was about to wrap a blanket around him. Would you have him freeze?'

'I would not be pushing and pulling at that leg, *amadán*! Leave him as he is and build up the fire instead.'

Tom was somewhere soft and grey, with occasional stars. He heard their voices as a distant buzz. In order to understand what they were saying he would have to move towards the pain. Or he could go in the other direction. Into a roaring darkness. Where there was no pain.

Probably no pain.

He decided to stay where he was for a while. Floating in the midst of nothing. On a great sea of nothingness ...

Roaringwater Bay sprang into his mind. The full glorious sweep of the bay glittering in the sunlight. Like an anchor, the image of the bay held him in place and kept him from drifting away.

* * *

After a brief but spirited argument about who was to go, Séamus left Seán to mind the children. The last thing he said as he went out the door was, 'Don't be touching him now, any of you.' He set off at a run.

Donal bent over Tom, who was lying on the floor in front of the fire. 'Séamus will bring my parents. They'll know what to do. Mother's a healer.'

'Your father's the king,' Tom mumbled.

'That's right! Can you hear me?'

Tom did not answer.

Donal felt guilty for being jealous of his friend. He wanted to do something – anything – to help Tom, if only to give him a drink of water. But he did not dare disobey his uncle.

Maura only obeyed orders she liked. She began to dance around the bed, singing fanciful spells and waving her hands above Tom. Once or twice she almost brushed him with her fingertips.

Seán reproved her. 'Do not be hurting him now.'

'I'm helping him. I'm a healer too.' As if to stake her claim, she put one hand on his forearm.

'No doctor!' Tom cried out. He sounded terrified.

By the time Séamus arrived with Bríd and Muiris, Tom was asleep. The pain was making him restless. Bríd examined him as gently as she could without waking him. 'His leg is broken,' she reported. 'Not a bad break, the bone has not come through the skin. He should be with his own family, though. His poor mother will be worried to distraction.'

Donal asked, 'What can she do that you can't?'

'She will send for a doctor,' said Muiris.

'No doctor!' Maura cried. 'Tomflynn said no doctor. He's afeared of doctor, whatever that is.'

Tom swam up from his troubled sleep. 'Doctors make it worse,' he said.

Muiris crouched down beside the bed. 'You are injured, Tomás. If Donal or Maura were injured–'

'My mother mended my arm when I broke it,' Donal interrupted. 'She pulled it hard – that hurt something terrible but I didn't cry – then she spread a paste on it and wrapped it in red flannel.' He thrust the arm close to Tom's face. 'Look, you can't even see where the break was.'

Muiris pushed Donal aside. 'The night has come and there is a storm, Tomás. I fear it would not be safe to carry you home now, either on a litter or in a currach.'

Carry me home. Muiris and Séamus, probably. My mother will see them. There will be questions. She will tell Father. 'I don't want to go, Muiris. Can't I stay here? I won't be any trouble.'

Muiris cocked an eyebrow at his wife. 'Tomás says he will not be any trouble.'

'In what lifetime will that be?' she asked with a wry smile. 'You should not have let him come here the first time.'

'How could I refuse?'

During the night Tom tossed and turned, but only with the upper part of his body. If any movement reached his leg, the pain woke him. In order to escape he sank back into the soft greyness amid the stars.

He was unaware that he called out a name.

Maura heard him, though. Several times during the night the little girl had crept silently down the ladder and tiptoed across the earthen floor to peer into the bedroom. To be certain Tom was really there.

She woke Donal. 'Tomflynn wants his mother,' she whispered.

Donal replied, 'I don't blame him.' He turned over and tried to go back to sleep.

Maura was relentless. 'He doesn't want to go to that house.'

'What can I do about it?'

'We can go there, Don-don. You and me. We can 'splain to his mother so she will let him stay with us. Don't you want him to stay?'

By now Donal was fully awake.

CHAPTER SIXTEEN

• • • • • • • • • •

DONAL AND MAURA GO ON A MISSION

Catherine Flynn awoke with a start.

Eithne stood beside the bed. Her woollen night cap was askew. 'Master Tom did not come home last night, madam.'

Mrs Flynn sat up. 'Where is he? What could have happened?'

'I don't know,' the former nurse said. 'I didn't see him leave.'

'Did anyone else see him?'

'Not to my knowledge.'

'How can my son leave this house without anyone knowing?'

'Master Tom comes and goes as he pleases,' Eithne informed her.

'When did that start?'

'In the summer, I believe it was.'

'And no one told me?'

Eithne hesitated, unwilling to make any dangerous admissions. 'We thought you knew.'

Catherine Flynn searched her memory. Were there clues she had overlooked? Had she been too busy with her own problems to pay attention? Her daughters were easy enough, she understood women. But Tom was a boy and she had never understood men. She hated to ask the next question. 'Has Tom stayed out all night before?'

'Not to my knowledge.'

The household was alerted. The women ran through the house, calling into rooms, opening cupboards. Simon, who had mournful brown eyes like a hound puppy, organised the other men to search outside.

As the sun was rising they made a discovery – but it was not Tom.

Simon hurried to tell Mrs Flynn. 'We found these rascals skulking in the grounds,' he said. He was gripping the arm of a sinewy boy. The boy's other hand was clutched by a small girl.

The boy was flushed with anger, but the girl gave a crow of delight. 'I know you! You're Tomflynn's mother!'

Before she could stop herself Mrs Flynn exclaimed, 'I know you too!'

Maura glanced up at her brother. 'See? I told you.'

Simon struggled to keep his face expressionless in this

extraordinary situation. 'What shall I do with them, madam?'

'Leave them with me, Simon, it will be all right.'

'If they make any trouble—'

'They will not make any trouble,' she said. After he left the room she voiced the questions that were bursting out of her. 'Who are you, why are you here, and do you know where Tom is? My little boy?'

'Tomflynn hurted hisself and—'

Donal put his hand over Maura's mouth. 'Tomás had a bad fall, but my mother is a healer and she's caring for him. As soon as he feels better we'll bring him home.'

Maura fought free of the brotherly restraint. 'I'm Maura,' she said, answering the first question. 'And this is Don-don.'

'Donal,' her brother corrected. 'I am called Donal.'

Mrs Flynn raised her eyebrows. 'Donal what? What is your surname — your last name?'

'Ó Driscoll.'

The woman closed her eyes. Opened them again. Looked from Donal to his sister and back to him. 'Yes,' she said softly. And again, 'Yes.'

Donal's curious eyes wandered around the great hall. Noticing the dark, heavy furniture. The bashed-in chest. The chairs disfigured by clumsy repairs. The Persian rug.

Maura tugged at his hand. 'I told you!' she insisted. 'I told you it's fancy. I was here, I saw ev'ryfing.'

Mrs Flynn gave herself a shake like someone waking from

a dream. 'Indeed you were here, Maura. Did I think to invite you back?'

Maura stared up with huge blue eyes. 'What's a 'vite?'

'Good manners.'

'What's manners?'

Donal warned, 'If you let her ask questions she'll never stop.'

Mrs Flynn nodded. 'My Tom is like that.'

'He is like that,' Donal agreed.

Catherine Flynn's knees felt weak. She looked around for the nearest chair and sank onto it. A chair leg creaked a warning.

'I can mend that for you,' offered Donal.

She was aware that the servants, and probably her daughters as well, were hovering just out of sight. Listening. She made an effort to raise her voice. 'We need a pitcher of milk, and some bread and butter. And honey; bring a little pot of honey.' She turned to Maura. 'You do like honey? I loved it when I was your age.'

Maura's eyes shone like stars.

While the children ate – sitting crosslegged at her feet, because they refused the chairs – she questioned them. Donal answered as best he could with a mouthful of food and frequent interruptions from Maura.

At last Mrs Flynn folded her hands and leaned back in her chair. The chair leg creaked again.

'I can mend anything,' Donal told her.

Her reply was almost too low for him to hear. 'Some things can never be mended.'

She called her daughters to join them. 'Tom has had an accident and broken his leg,' she announced. 'These children were kind enough to bring us the news.'

Virginia, who had a smudge of blue paint on her nose, said urgently, 'We must bring him home and send for a doctor straight away. Call Simon back and–'

Mrs Flynn was shaking her head. 'Tom won't have a doctor, and you know it. As for bringing him home, I think it best to leave him where he is for now.'

'We shall go to him, then.'

'No, Elizabeth!' Her daughters were startled by the unusual strength of their mother's voice. 'None of us are going to him.'

'Father would expect–'

'Your father is not here, Caroline. I make the decisions now, and I am making this one.'

The Flynn girls stared in astonishment at a mother they did not know.

* * *

Tom was awake. Looking up, he could just make out the underside of a thatched roof in the dim light. He heard the crackle of a fire on a hearth. His tongue felt thick and the inside of his mouth was numb.

Where am I? And what's wrong with me?

He thought back, step by step. Memory came slowly.

During the night Bríd had given him a drink which tasted the way ferns smelt. She had made him drain the cup. Afterwards ... no pain. Nothing.

He began to remember other, earlier things. Muiris holding him under the shoulders. Bríd's square, strong hands locking around his leg. Pain like the world splitting apart, and himself crying out.

'I see you are back with us,' Bríd said as she leaned over him. 'How do you feel?'

He licked his lips. They were cracked and dry. 'Thirsty,' he told her.

She brought him a cup of pure, sweet water, which he gratefully gulped down. It washed the last of the ferny taste from his mouth. 'Thank you,' he said. And then, because she was still watching him intently, he added, 'My leg aches.'

'Your leg aches because you fell and broke it, Tomás. We repaired the leg last night. You are young and strong; the bone will heal well.'

'When will it stop hurting?'

Bríd replied, 'The less you think about pain the sooner it will go away. That is what Muiris always says.'

'Is Muiris here?'

163

'He is not here, he went to look for Donal and Maura.'

'Were they injured too?'

'Not at all; they rescued you. But they slipped out while we were still asleep. Muiris thinks they went to tell your mother about your accident.'

Tom was dismayed. 'That's the last thing I want! To her I'm still a baby. If she knows what happened she will never let me come here again.'

* * *

At first no one else agreed with Mrs Flynn's decision. Elizabeth said they should pray for guidance before they did anything. Virginia suggested Mrs Flynn might be having 'an airy fit'. 'She was very ill for a while, remember? Illness takes people in their heads sometimes.'

That was enough to switch Caroline to her mother's side. 'There is nothing wrong with Mother's head! I don't know how you can say that, Ginny Flynn. You're just trying to make yourself seem more important. Mother would never do anything to hurt any of us. If she wants Tom to stay where he is for now, I am sure she has a good reason.'

'Like what?'

'I don't know, but I trust her. What do you think, Lizzie?'

Elizabeth looked from one of her sisters to the other. Virginia, so brisk and sure of herself, like their father. Caroline, so soft and gentle, like their mother. Yet obviously there was steel somewhere inside Caro.

There is steel in me too, Elizabeth decided. 'Ginny, you have no right to question any decision of Mother's. I shall trust her too. Keep your foolish opinions to yourself.'

No one had ever called Virginia foolish before.

* * *

Muiris returned to the cabin with Donal and Maura. 'Look what I found,' he said.

'They're soaking wet!' his wife scolded. 'Come over to the fire the pair of you, and get warm. And you, Muiris, a hot drink would do you no harm either.'

Tom propped himself up on one elbow. 'Did you see my mother? Did any of you see my mother?'

'I saw her,' Donal told him. His sister jabbed him with her elbow. 'We both saw her, Maura and me. She is a *lady*,' Donal added in an awed voice.

Tom looked anxiously toward Muiris, but the man was busy heating a kettle over the fire.

'And we saw your sisters,' Maura said, taking up the narrative. 'The big one sitted me on her lap and the little one gived me a ... a .... what did she gived me, Don-don?'

'A sweet biscuit.'

'A sweet bikkit.' Maura giggled. 'With a funny thing on it.

165

What was that?'

'The stamp of the Dutch East India Company,' Donal said. 'The lady explained it to me. There was a whole box of sweet biscuits but it was almost empty. We ate the last ones. The lady said we could.'

Tom wanted to shout at them, but he managed to sound almost calm when he asked Muiris, 'What did my mother have to say about me?'

CHAPTER SEVENTEEN

· · · · · · · · · · ·

ELIZABETH FINDS COURAGE

'I did not see your mother.' Muiris was answering Tom's question, but he was looking at Bríd as he spoke. 'The children were already on their way home when I met them.'

'Tomás can stay with us until he is stronger,' Donal announced. 'His mother told me so.'

'She told *me*,' Maura insisted.

'All right, she told you. But only because you kept on and on about it. You know how Maura is,' said Donal. 'Once she gets her teeth into something.'

Tom was amazed that his mother had given her permission. He knew it was only a temporary reprieve. When he was stronger – whenever that might be – he would have to face her. And if she was not furious when she found out about his summer's activities, his father certainly would be.

He could not even imagine what his father would do to

167

him. Unless, of course, something happened to his father in the meantime.

Which would be even worse.

Not so long ago, life had seemed simple. He had felt like a man. Now he was reduced to being a child again, and help-less.

Muiris asked, 'Why were you on the cliffs yesterday, Tomás?'

Yesterday seemed so long ago. It was hard to remember. There were no words for his feelings. 'I was coming here. I just wanted to be here.'

Muiris exchanged a look with his wife.

At midday Bríd gave him another cup of the ferny-tasting drink, and then some bread and cheese. He did not feel much like eating. Maura sat beside him and tore off bits of bread. Making little cooing sounds, she pressed them against his lips. When he laughed, she pushed them in.

Afterwards he felt drowsy. There was some pain but only at a distance; it did not really touch him. He closed his eyes for a minute.

When he opened them it was night again.

The cabin was filled with people. Seán and Séamus were there with most of the clan. No one noticed that Tom was awake, so he closed his eyes again and lay listening content-edly to the hum of their voices. The good-humoured banter, the earnest conversations, the silly jokes and colourful stories.

Tom understood more Irish than he would have a year

ago. Perhaps someone will sing, he thought hopefully.

His leg was not hurting. He was warm and comfortable and surrounded by friends. His very good friends. He would have to return to Roaringwater House eventually, but he did not want to think about that. He did not want to think at all, just drift and dream and pretend ... pretend he was home to stay.

The old man said sharply, 'You are playing with fire, Muiris.'

'When have I not?'

'This fire will burn you to a cinder. Mind what I tell you.'

'The matter was settled long ago.'

'We thought it was. You stir embers with a stick and they flare up again.'

Muiris said, 'The stick was not in my hand but in Donal's.'

'The child's hand, the man's arm,' the old woman intoned.

The conversations faded away. Or Tom faded away. Into a pleasant dream of sunlight glittering on the bay and a soft wind blowing. The voices of people became the voices of seabirds.

On the following morning Bríd unwrapped Tom's leg. With a dry muslin cloth she gently wiped away the thick paste that covered it. 'This was made from comfrey,' she explained as she worked.

They examined the leg together. 'It's all shrivelled,' Tom said worriedly.

'It is shrivelled,' the woman agreed, 'but that is from the binding, not the break. There is no swelling, and see how straight the bone lies. Now you must drink a decoction of comfrey. Then we can wrap you up again.'

The decoction of comfrey was more bitter than the ferny drink. Tom made a face. 'Isn't anything else good for broken bones?'

'Many things, Tomás. For a person your age and a break like this, I use comfrey inside and out.'

'At least you don't bleed me.'

She looked at him in horror.

When the leg was tightly wrapped she gave the boy a stout blackthorn stick to lean upon and allowed him to hobble about the cabin. 'Do not hit that leg against anything,' she warned.

'Believe me, I don't want to.'

Donal and Maura had been sent outside while their mother worked on Tom's leg. Now the little girl came running in. 'Tomflynn's all well!' she chirped. She was about to throw her arms around him when Bríd stopped her. 'Be as careful with him as with a bird's egg, *a mhúirnín*,' she warned the child.

'Is he still broken?'

'Not broken, but not mended either.'

Maura bunched up her forehead in a small child's version of a frown. 'He must be one or the other.'

'There is an in-between place, too,' said her mother. 'A lot of time is spent in in-between places.'

Maura looked Tom up and down. 'When you're not 'tween will ye play with me again?'

'You can count on it!' he promised.

Tom's delight at being up did not last long. He tired quickly, and soon was ready to go back to bed. The leg ached. Bríd gave him a delicious pudding made from carrageen moss and honey, then more of the ferny drink. He went to sleep before the sun did.

Next morning he felt – almost – like his old self. In a few more days he would be well able to return to Roaringwater House. He did not suggest this to anyone. Nor did anyone mention it to him. The temporary bed that had been made up for him in the cabin remained. The blankets were aired, but never folded and put away.

Bríd gave him a homespun tunic and a woollen coat to wear. 'These were Seán's,' she said, 'when he was your size. There are some woollen trews as well, but we don't want to put them over your leg.'

As Tom's strength returned he made himself useful. There was always work to be done, work which did not require two sound legs. He opened oysters, he gutted and scaled fish, he sharpened knives and plaited rope and mended baskets.

'Pleasant it is,' Bríd remarked, 'to have a man's help inside the house as well as outside.'

As soon as my leg heals I can do a man's work outside, Tom thought with satisfaction.

Yet Roaringwater House remained on the horizon of his mind like a storm at sea waiting to blow in.

In their bed at night Bríd and Muiris discussed him in hushed voices. 'We cannot keep Tomás forever,' she reminded her husband.

'The boy is making good progress,' he replied, 'but healing cannot be hurried, you know yourself. When the time is right we will take him home.'

'Who will take him?'

'I will, Bríd.'

'There is no need for you to go. Send Fergal instead.'

'What sort of chieftain lets others do the hard things for him?'

Bríd gave a wifely sigh. 'Your uncle was right, Muiris. You are playing with fire.'

* * *

Catherine Flynn ordered the servants to set a place for Tom at every meal. Simon and the other male servants were under strict orders to keep a watch out for him.

'I do not understand you, Mother,' Virginia complained. 'I simply do not understand your abandoning Tom to strangers.'

When Herbert Fox arrived to pay a call on Elizabeth, she told him what she knew of the situation. Fox, a grizzled man with yellowed teeth and sour breath, was as puzzled as the girls. 'Why have you not sent someone to fetch the boy home long before this?' he asked Catherine Flynn.

'A broken leg can take a long time to heal,' she said. 'Tom is being well minded where he is, and does not have stairs to climb.'

'Where *is* he exactly, Mrs Flynn?'

She would not meet his eyes. 'Not far away. Among friends.'

'Your mother will not give me any direct answers,' Fox told Tom's sisters. 'I am convinced that something is wrong. I shall send my own men to bring him home. It is my duty to your family, Elizabeth.'

Elizabeth drew a deep breath. Her clenched fists were hidden in the folds of her skirt. 'We appreciate your concern, Mr Fox, but you are not yet part of this family. I think it best if we accept our mother's decision.'

After he left the room Virginia broke into laughter. 'I cannot believe you defied him, Lizzie!'

'My knees were shaking,' her sister admitted. 'But I am so tired of always doing what some man tells me. Besides, he could not find Tom anyway unless Mother told him where to look.'

Caroline said, 'Do you think she knows?'

'I am certain of it.'

My dearest Kate,

Thomas Wentworth was created Earl of Strafford on the 12th of January and appointed Lord Lieutenant of Ireland on the 13th of January. His new position gives him complete dominion over this island, second only to the king. I have hitched my wagon to a shooting star! I remain here in Dublin awaiting his triumphal return. While I wait I am making some new financial arrangements in anticipation of the future. A bright future it will be for all of us, Kate. I promise.

• • • • • • • • •

CHAPTER EIGHTEEN

THE END OF WINTER

Epiphany came and went. St Brigid's Day approached. The weather was as cold as ever but the daylight lasted longer. Tom's leg itched unbearably. He could not stop clawing at the bindings. Every time Bríd changed them he begged her to leave them off entirely.

One morning she said, 'If your leg was not bound, Tomás, could you walk unaided?'

'I could of course.'

'Then you are ready to go home. Young bones mend quickly.'

'I mean, I think I can walk. But maybe not. I'm sure I'll still need the stick.'

Bríd's eyes danced with amusement. 'Do you want me to re-bind your leg after all?'

'Yes, please,' he said, embarrassed to be caught out.

That night on the pillow they shared, Bríd told Muiris, 'The time is right. We cannot keep Tomás away from his own family any longer.'

175

CAVE OF SECRETS

Her husband lay silent in the darkness. She listened to his breathing until she fell asleep.

The following morning he asked Tom to come outside with him. The boy was delighted, thinking he was going to help Muiris. One look at the man's serious expression in the daylight told him otherwise.

'You are happy with us, Tomás, and we are happy with you. Never doubt that.'

Tom's heart sank. 'You're going to send me home, aren't you? Please, for my sake, let me stay. For another week?'

'For your sake I would,' Muiris replied. 'This is for the sake of someone else. Tomorrow I will take you in the currach.'

Tom made a deliberate effort to enjoy his last day with them. But he felt like a traitor. Now that it was a certainty, he had to admit to himself that part of him really did want to go home. To see his mother and his sisters again, to sleep in his own bed-closet and eat the sort of food he had eaten all his life.

When it was time to leave, Donal and Maura accompanied him to the boat. The little girl had tears in her eyes. 'You'll come back soon, Tomflynn?'

'I will of course.'

Donal held out a closed fist. When he turned it over and opened it, a striped sea shell lay on his palm. 'This is the shell you found,' he told Tom. 'The first day the three of us were together.'

'It's Tomflynn's 'pology!' Maura exclaimed.

'Take it with you,' said Donal.

'I gave it to you, it's yours now.'

'Bring it back to me when you come.'

As the currach pulled away from the shore Tom looked back at them. He felt an awful ache in his throat.

'Would you like to help me row, Tomás?'

'Yes, please!'

Seen from the water, the cove appeared smaller than he remembered. Nor was the cliff above as steep. 'There is a sort of path behind those rocks,' Tom told Muiris. 'It's easier than it looks. I think I can get to the top by myself.'

The man ignored him. Rowing to water's edge, he jumped out and pulled the currach onto the beach. 'Help me turn this over, Tomás.'

Muiris went straight to the foot of the hidden path as if he knew where it was. 'Bring your stick,' he called to the surprised boy.

As they neared the top Tom said, 'I can go on from here, Muiris.'

'So can I.'

They set off across the windswept earth together.

A mile was a greater distance than Tom remembered. He leaned on the stick, but soon that was not enough. Muiris knew before he did. He swooped the boy into his arms and carried him until they were in sight of Roaringwater House.

'You might want to walk from here, Tomás. In case anyone sees.'

'Are you going back now?'

Muiris squared his shoulders. 'I am not going back now.'

They marched to the front door together.

Virginia and her mother were in the hall, discussing possible repairs for the Persian rug. 'There is no one in Munster who could mend it properly,' Mrs Flynn declared.

'Then let me try.'

'Your pride outruns your ability, Virginia. One mistake could ruin it forever. Then what would your father say? No, I think the best thing to do is to send the rug to Dublin.'

'Will that not be expensive?'

'Very, I suspect. But it will be a nice surprise for your father when he comes home. And we should be able to afford it by then,' she added.

A powerful fist pounded on the front door. Both women gave a start. Mrs Flynn glanced around for a servant to answer the summons, but there was none in the hall. She went to the door herself. Virginia followed her.

The heavy door creaked on its iron hinges. The woman said over her shoulder, 'We must have this oiled before—'

She stopped. Put one hand to her throat.

'*Dia dhuit, a Chaitríona,*' said Muiris Ó Driscoll.

Virginia edged past her mother, who seemed to have grown roots where she stood. 'There you are at last, Tom!

Come into the house at once. You gave us such a fright!'
Without glancing at his companion, she flung her arms
around her brother and gave him a hug. Then she swept him
into the house and shouted for her sisters.

Catherine and Muiris stood looking at each other.

CHAPTER NINETEEN

A REUNION

'I did not expect you,' Catherine Flynn said faintly.

'Tomás is not strong enough yet to come by him-self.'

With the ghost of a smile, she replied, 'It is not such a great distance.'

'No,' he agreed, 'not such a great distance.'

'But too far for you until now.' There was reproach in her voice.

He did not respond.

'Not too far for your children, though,' she went on. 'They are yours, are they not? Donal and little Maura?'

'They are mine.'

'You can be proud of them, Muiris.'

'I am,' he said. 'As you are proud of Tomás and your three daughters.'

'How did you know I have three daughters?'

'Two are pretty,' Muiris went on, 'and one, I believe, is clever. Cleverness lasts longer than beauty, Caitríona.'

180

Her hand flew to her cheek.

'Who is this person?' Elizabeth demanded to know. 'Are you one of the villains who kidnapped my brother? Father said there were pirates in the bay, but I never–'

Mrs Flynn turned away from Muiris, saying, 'I want to see my boy.' When she hurried into the hall, he followed her.

They found Tom sitting on a chair, with Virginia and Caroline standing on either side of him. They were doing the talking, their words overlapping one another in their excitement. In the shadowy room the boy looked pale. The walking stick was propped beside him.

His mother's eyes went straight to the stick. 'So you did break your leg. Oh, my poor baby!'

'Stupid of me,' said Tom. 'I was running and slipped on the ice. I fell down a hill. Or off of a hill, I'm not sure what happened exactly.'

'What were you running from?' Elizabeth asked.

'I wasn't running from anything, Lizzie. I was going to visit my ...' Tom met Muiris's eyes. Those intense eyes that could see right through him. 'My friends. My best friends. They took care of me until I was able to come home again.'

His mother looked around for a chair so she could sit down too. She felt faint but she refused to give in to it. My people do not faint, she told herself.

She beckoned to Muiris to come and stand beside her. His eyes asked a question; she answered it with a nod. She took his hand. Held it tight. 'This man is more than a friend,' she said. Reaching down inside herself for the voice she had submerged for so long, the confident voice with the accents of the Gael. It was rusty from disuse, but she forced it into her throat. 'This is your uncle.' The voice grew stronger. 'My oldest brother, Muiris Ó Driscoll of Roaringwater Bay.'

Caroline gasped.

'That's impossible!' cried Elizabeth. 'We cannot be related to *pirates!*'

Muiris said with quiet dignity, 'I am not a pirate. Even if I were, I would not apologise for it. Piracy is a respectable profession – from time to time. The English queen knighted her favourite pirates. Have you heard of Sir Walter Raleigh? Sir Francis Drake? Or Sir Fineen Ó Driscoll , the greatest of them all?'

Tom's sisters struggled with their shock. Their mother made it worse by bursting into laughter. 'Muiris, you have not changed a peg.'

He raised one eyebrow. 'Did you think I would?'

She stopped laughing. 'No. I did not think you would change.'

'You changed, Caitríona.' He made it sound like an accusation.

Tom and his sisters looked from one to the other, trying to make sense of their conversation.

'I had to change, Muiris. To live this life, I had to become the woman I am now.'

He scowled. 'You did not have to live this life. You had a choice.'

'*A chroí!* From the day I first saw William I had no choice. And he felt the same way. Father understood. That is why he agreed to my dowry.'

'Which impoverished the rest of us, and built this monstrosity of a house!' Muiris said angrily, snatching his hand away from hers. 'Has any of it made you happy, Caitríona?'

'My children make me happy.' The soft voice again. The lowered eyelids.

Elizabeth said, 'I do not understand. Did *you* pay for Roaringwater House, Mother?'

The voice became a whisper. 'William built it with my marriage portion.'

Virginia said, 'You were right, Lizzie. We *are* traded like animals. How large a dowry do you suppose Father offered Mr Fox to take you off his hands?'

Elizabeth went white.

'Stop this!' cried Tom. 'You're tearing at one another!'

Muiris looked down at his sister. 'After this house was built there would not have been much left of your dowry, Caitríona. Not enough to buy fine clothes and furnishings. The land itself is barren; only sheep and goats can survive on it, and not many of either. How does Liam Ó Floinn support you?'

'He has investments, I believe. Something about the East India Company? We never discuss it, though. William says I could not understand finance.'

Her brother's expression softened. 'Oh my poor Cáit. What has your wilfulness cost you? Your son is right, he is a wise boy. We are tearing ourselves apart over a war that was won and lost long ago.'

Tom felt as if a bag had been opened in front of him and its contents spilt out on the flagstones. Not shining gold ingots, but dark secrets dredged up from the bottom of a black sea. He wanted to be anywhere else but here. 'Take me home with you, Muiris? Please, please take me home!'

'You are home, Tomás,' said Muiris. Looking at Catherine Flynn, he added, 'You have to live your own life. I cannot give you a different one.'

She wilted under his gaze. 'Are you abandoning me again, Muiris?'

'I never abandoned you. When your husband was away I sometimes came near the house, hoping to catch a glimpse of you. And your children.'

'I never saw you.'

'You never looked for me.'

'*I* did,' Elizabeth said unexpectedly. 'I was not looking for *you*, exactly, but for someone. I desperately wanted someone. – anyone – a prince to rescue me, or God to make everything all right for me. Someone.'

Her mother turned towards her in astonishment.

Seizing his opportunity, Muiris gave Tom's shoulder a quick squeeze and strode from the hall – and the house – before anyone could stop him.

* * *

Mrs Flynn retired to her chamber. She called for a cloth soaked in lavender water to place on her forehead, and said she did not want to be disturbed.

Tom's sisters descended on him like a flock of seagulls on a fish carcass. 'Is he really our uncle?' 'How did you find him?' 'Does he have a family?' 'Is that where you were going last summer?'

Muiris only answers the questions he want to answer, Tom reminded himself. 'My leg hurts,' he told his sisters. 'I want my bed now. Will one of you help me up the stairs?'

When he was in his bed-closet with the panel firmly closed – and the questions shut outside – he tried to put the pieces together in his head. This was like one of Seán's colourful tales about the Milesians or the Tuatha dé Danann, a tapestry woven of many threads. Yet this tale was true. And the threads led to him.

Does every family have secrets? Are all children as ignorant as I was of the astonishing past which produced me?

CHAPTER TWENTY

THE RETURN OF MR FLYNN

Roaringwater House was turned upside down. The appearance of Muiris had been like a thunderbolt. The servants talked of nothing else. There was excited whispering in the kitchen and chattering on the back stairs. Some claimed they knew everything. Others said they knew nothing but were eager to be informed. One or two merely smiled and kept their mouths shut.

Mrs Flynn emerged from her room the following morning, but she discouraged conversation and would not talk about her brother at all. Tom also evaded his sisters' questions. He used his leg as an excuse, though he was no longer in pain. Bríd was a true healer, much better than the barber/doctor from Ballydehob.

The boy wanted time by himself to sort out his thoughts. He wished it were summer so he could go swimming. The days were gradually growing longer, but the water was still very cold and he did not trust his leg.

He tried to be satisfied with looking out the little window in his room, gazing towards the bay.

I have the threads, he thought, but I don't see the whole pattern. Am I related to Fineen Ó Driscoll? Was he my grandfather? My great grandfather? Is his blood in my veins at all?

Tom wanted to know and was afraid to know. Afraid of being disappointed by the answer.

During the next few nights he had nightmares, though they were not the same as before. Now they featured a face-less man dressed in brocades and high leather boots. He carried a great, curving sword with a hilt of gold. Sometimes the man threatened Tom with the sword. In other dreams he gave the sword to the boy as a gift.

The thunder of hoofbeats on the frozen carriage road broke the spell which had fallen over Roaringwater House. Within moments they heard shouting, then Simon's cry, 'The master's home!'

William Flynn had not returned alone. He was mounted on a superb new horse and accompanied by four other men who were equally well mounted. They all wore new clothing, if travel-stained, and had plumes in their hats.

Flynn tossed his reins to the stable boy and slid from the saddle as if he did not ache in every bone and joint. His wife and children hurried to greet him. During the months of his absence Tom's vivid imagination had pictured far too many tragic scenes involving William Flynn. Now here was the man himself, thankfully alive and well. Though a bit thinner.

'William!' his wife exclaimed, aghast. 'Have they fed you nothing in Dublin?'

'On the contrary, I ate very well,' he assured her. 'Do we not eat well, men?' he asked his four companions.

They laughed and nodded. With an extravagant wave of his arm, Flynn ushered them into his house. His magnificent Roaringwater House, created through his own cleverness. Safe now, thanks to his courage and persistence. He felt wonderful. In the glow of his mood even his son was a welcome sight. 'Look at you, boy! I wager you have grown two years' worth in half a year!' Flynn gave Tom a fatherly punch on the arm.

The boy blinked in surprise.

Flynn kissed his wife on the cheek and hugged each of his daughters in turn. 'I have presents for all of you,' he said. 'New Year's presents, even if they are a little late. But welcome anyway, eh? Eh?'

His family nodded in unison. They were watching him in fascination. With the exception of his wife, none of them had ever seen William Flynn exuberant.

He introduced his four companions as 'members of my company' and called for tankards of beer to be served to them immediately.

The men took over the great hall as if they were holding court. They threw off their travelling cloaks and tossed them to Simon. He neatly folded all five, though he did not look happy. Caring for the outerwear of strangers was beneath his rank in the hierarchy of servants.

Catherine Flynn eyed her husband's clothes. 'I do not remember that coat and those breeches, William.'

'These?' He made a dismissive gesture. 'They are only temporary until the earl can have proper uniforms made for us.'

She raised her eyebrows. 'The Earl of Cork?'

'Of course not, woman! The Earl of Strafford, Lord Lieutenant Thomas Wentworth. In April the king will summon the English parliament to raise more money for the war against the Scottish rebels. Meanwhile Strafford has returned to Ireland to organise an army of Irish soldiers. He is confident he can convince the Irish parliament to provide the funds.

'I was one of the first to greet him upon his arrival. I hired a trumpeter out of my own pocket and arranged for a small but elegant refreshment to be served at dockside. Very expensive, of course, but a worthwhile investment. I do not think he expected such a warm reception. He certainly showed his gratitude. On his instructions I am to recruit soldiers in Cork.'

'Does this mean you have your commission, William?'

He beamed. 'I do indeed. I am a major in Strafford's army.

These men with me are my senior officers. I shall be equipping them myself until our funds come through, but then I shall be repaid with interest. We are going to Scotland to fight for the king!'

Tom made his first mistake of the day. 'What king?'

'King Charles, of course, our lawful sovereign. What's the matter with you, boy? Are you simple?' Forgotten was the warm greeting, the fond punch on the arm. William Flynn's familiar scowl returned.

Tom slipped out of the hall as soon as he could and went to his chamber.

There are other kings, he thought as he gazed out the window towards the bay. There are Irish kings to whom Irish men should owe their loyalty.

Loyalty was a slippery subject. The more Tom thought about it, the less certain he was about his own. Perhaps one had to be an adult to understand. Yet I am an adult when I'm with Muiris and his family. And they are my blood kin. But so are my parents.

I love Muiris. But perhaps I would love my father if he would let me.

Tom's head began to ache. He longed to crawl into his bed-closet and shut the panel on his problems. That was not the sort of thing a man would do, however.

Squaring his shoulders, Tom went back downstairs.

Virginia beckoned to him. 'Cook's been told to prepare a

huge dinner and Father's taken his friends out to inspect the
stables. How many men make up a company, Tom? As many
as a regiment?'

'I don't think so. I don't really know.'

'Neither do I. I *hate* living in such an isolated place. We are
kept in perfect ignorance. Like the situation with Mother's
brother. Do you really believe that—'

'I have a message for Cook,' Tom interrupted, hastily head-
ing for the back stairs. It need not be a lie. He could tell the
cook that he would not be taking dinner with the rest of
them.

In the passage at the bottom of the back stairs he found
the members of his father's 'company'. They filled the space
with their presence, talking loudly and stamping mud off
their boots. They ignored Tom as he politely tried to edge
past them.

One man said disdainfully, 'Only a handful of saddle horses
and none I would care to ride.'

'The brown gelding is herring-gutted,' another commented. 'They all show too much daylight beneath.'

'Did you note the mismatched carriage horses?' asked a
third. 'Or the ancient pony with hipbones like a hatrack?
What does the major feed those nags on? Gorse?'

'Do you mean furze?' Tom asked.

The men laughed.

Tom faced them squarely. 'My father has the best horses

on the bay,' he declared.

'Best what? Seahorses?' Now the men were laughing at him.

'Since you obviously don't know,' Tom said coldly, 'furze makes excellent fodder. You chop off the green tops and pound them on a flat surface with a mallet. Horses thrive on it.'

He stalked away before they could think of a reply.

His father was still at the stables, talking to the groom. Flynn was doing most of the talking. The groom listened with averted eyes and a bored expression. From time to time he responded with a grunt, which his master could take any way he liked.

As Tom approached, Flynn noticed his son's walking stick for the first time. 'What did you do to your leg, boy?'

'I had a fall, but I'm all right.'

'You always were clumsy,' said Flynn. Stroking his lower lip, he surveyed his son. 'You have grown since I saw you last, boy. What age are you now?'

'Fourteen next month, sir.'

'Is that all? You look older now. In Dublin I met a lad only a year or so older than you who is a man in every way. He was of great help to me, in fact.'

'I'm glad to hear it, sir.'

'Fourteen, eh?'

'Yes, sir.' Tom felt himself begin to sweat, though the day

was cold. This was leading somewhere. He tried to be prepared.

'What are we to do with you in another year, boy?'

Tom did not reply. He knew from experience that anything he said might only add fuel to the fire.

'Young men of fifteen march with armies,' Flynn commented. 'Fifteen may be the best age for a soldier; they are full of vigour then. Would you like to be a soldier? If you live long enough you might even become an officer someday. Or perhaps you would rather be a scholar like my friend in Dublin? Probably not, though,' he continued, answering his own question. 'Scholars need brains and I have never seen any evidence of yours. I am wasting money on that wretch Beasley.'

Tom knew his father did not care what he wanted. He stood straight and silent – and sweating – while William Flynn peered at him from beneath his brows.

The boy is growing up, the man told himself. There was a time when he would cringe before me like a hound that expects to be beaten. I see no cringing in him now.

Dismissing Tom with a wave of his hand, Flynn resumed his one-sided conversation with the head groom. Out of the corner of his eye he watched his son walk away. Noticed how careful Tom was not to limp.

That lad might make a soldier, he might indeed, Flynn told himself. A soldier to fight for the king.

CHAPTER TWENTY-ONE

• • • • • • • • • •

OFF TO WAR

William Flynn and his men remained at Roaringwater House only for a few days before they galloped away again, full of high spirits. Tom watched them go with mixed feelings. His father's attitude towards him had changed a little. Sometimes it was almost pleasant. There had been too much talk of soldiers and war, however. His father had even asked the head groom to teach him to ride. 'If young Tom is meant for the cavalry we had best get to work right away, eh?'

Not once had Flynn asked how Tom had injured his leg, or how the boy felt. About anything.

As soon as his leg was strong enough, Tom set out for the narrow valley. He carried the walking stick but tried not to use it more than absolutely necessary. His friends – relatives! – greeted him warmly. Bríd was eager to see how well his leg was healing.

'We wondered if we would ever see you here again,' Muiris told him.

'Why would I not come?'

'Your parents could have stopped you.'

'My mother saw me leaving the house this morning and said nothing, though I'm sure she knew I was coming here. As for my father … he was home for a brief while but has gone again. I did not tell him about you, and I don't think my mother did either. He only cares about his own business anyway.'

Muiris said, 'And this business of his – is it so interesting?'

While Tom related what he knew of his father's plans, his uncle listened intently. 'So Thomas Wentworth is Lord Lieutenant now,' he said, 'and Liam Ó Floinn is in his camp. Liam probably believes he is safely nestled in the English king's pocket.'

His choice of words warned Tom. 'Is my father not safe with Thomas Wentworth? He has given him an officer's commission.'

'I am sure your father has a splendid commission, and gold braid for his coat,' Muiris said sarcastically. 'Fineen Ó Driscoll had a knighthood from the English crown, and much good it did him. The *Sasanach* used Fineen for as long as suited their purpose, then cut him loose with every Irishman's hand raised against him. His own son, Conor, had rebelled against him. The old man was forced to sell everything he owned. In the end he died penniless, with no one to tie up his jaw.

'Believe me when I tell you: a man who can be ennobled at the whim of an English monarch can lose his nobility just as quickly. You are far safer leaning on your blackthorn stick, Tomás, than your father will ever be leaning on the *Sasanach*.'

Tom spent the day with Donal and his family in the narrow valley. For long stretches of time it was as wonderful as he remembered. Then, like dark clouds passing across the face of the sun, his worries returned. The complicated adult world into which his father had ridden was like the swarming sea life beneath the surface of Roaringwater Bay. Unseen, unsuspected, unknowable.

But he was close to it now. He already had one foot in it. He could not go back to being a child even if he wanted to. Nor did he know how to take the next step.

His mother was waiting for him when he returned home. 'You were with Muiris,' she said.

'I was.'

'You have lost a lot of time with your studies, Tom, so I have sent for Mr Beasley to resume your lessons next week. Otherwise you will be studying right through the summer.'

'Are you trying to keep me from being with my uncle and his family?'

She looked hurt. 'I would not do that, Tom. I am glad you found one another. I kept that secret too long.'

'Why did you? Are you ashamed of them?'

Catherine Flynn lifted her head. 'Just the opposite, I am

proud of them. I am only ashamed that I did not appreciate what I had.'

'Does Father know about Muiris?'

'He knew from the beginning. I would never keep a secret from him. William looked down on the Irish who had not adopted English ways, but my family still had some money then, which made them more acceptable. I did not learn until too late that they used the last of it for my dowry. I felt so guilty I could not face them any more.'

'I'll take you to them tomorrow!' Tom said eagerly. 'They will be glad to see you.'

'They will not be glad. They hate me and I do not blame them.'

'If they hated you, Muiris would not have come here,' Tom pointed out. 'Nor would he have kept an eye on you all these years. Please, Mother, let me take you to them. They have the nicest little house, so warm and snug, and the morning sun comes in the windows.'

'I know,' she said. So softly he did not hear.

'They will make you welcome as they always do me and we can heal the damage that's been done. Bríd is a wonderful healer, just look what she did for my leg.'

'A broken leg is not the same as a broken family, Tom. We Irish carry our injuries to the grave.'

It was the first time Tom had ever heard his mother say 'we Irish'.

'It doesn't have to be that way!' he protested. 'I know it doesn't. Please say you'll come with me tomorrow, I know the way.'

'I know the way too,' Catherine Flynn replied.

This time he heard her.

* * *

In the morning it was raining. 'I shall have to wait for another day,' Mrs Flynn said at breakfast. She sounded relieved.

'If we don't go now you'll never go.'

'Of course I shall, Tom.'

Virginia spoke up. 'I think we should all go together, as I said last night. They are part of our family too.'

'We cannot pay a call in weather like this!' Caroline protested.

'The weather is always like this,' said Elizabeth. 'We live on Roaringwater Bay, remember? We can wrap up warmly and wear heavy boots.'

'That will not be necessary,' Mrs Flynn told them. 'This time I think it should only be Tom and myself.'

Tom reached across the table and seized his mother's hands. 'This time? Then you *are* going!'

'I have not yet decided if–'

'Say you will. Please?' The eyes gazing at her so earnestly were his father's eyes; William's eyes as Catherine remembered them, when he and she were young. How could she refuse those eyes anything? 'I shall go,' she said at last.

Warm outer clothing was gathered with a sense of urgency. Tom was afraid that if he wasted any time his mother would lose her nerve. Elizabeth and Virginia clamoured to accompany them, but Mrs Flynn would not allow it. What she was about to do would take all the courage she had. If she were rejected, she did not want her daughters as witnesses.

They made slow progress, the woman in her heavy cloak and the boy with his walking stick. For once there was little wind off the bay, but the rain pounded like a fist on their heads and shoulders. Where the going was rough Tom held his mother's arm. He threw down the stick because it got in his way.

'It's a strange thing,' he remarked to her. 'Sometimes it takes forever to reach the valley, and other times I come upon it long before I expect to.'

She said nothing.

Tom did not take a wrong turning. He found the marsh at the river mouth just where it should be, and led his mother to the narrow valley without mishap. The familiar cabins were waiting for them, snugly huddled under their thatch, their limewashed walls gleaming in the grey light.

Mrs Flynn stopped walking. 'They have not changed,' she said in a voice full of wonder. 'Everything else has changed, but not ...' She began to cry.

CHAPTER TWENTY-TWO
• • • • • • • • • •

MRS FLYNN PAYS A VISIT

Bríd had a pile of mending on her lap when she heard the knock on the door. 'Who but a fisherman would be out in this weather?' she muttered to herself. 'And I after telling himself we already have enough dried and salted fish to last until the summer, but would he listen? Not Muiris; not when there's something troubling his mind. Then he has to be busy.'

She raised her voice. 'The door's not latched, come in!'

The knock was repeated.

She thrust her needle through the topmost garment and set the pile aside. 'Have ye gone deaf?' she asked as she opened the door. 'Tomás, lad! Come into this house, you're very welcome.'

He did not step inside. 'My mother is with me, and she's crying. I can't get her to come any farther.'

Looking past him through a curtain of rain, Bríd saw

a woman muffled in a heavy cloak. She was bent almost double, with her two hands over her face. Bríd ran to her. 'Help me, Tomás!' With one on one side and one on the other, they walked Catherine Flynn through the open doorway and into the cabin.

'Sit by the hearth and warm yourself,' Bríd said. 'Och, look at the state of you, you could have come from the bottom of the bay. Take off that wet cloak at once.' She tried to fold Catherine's hood back.

'Leave me,' Tom's mother moaned. 'Please leave me be.'

Bríd pulled the hood away. 'Caitríona? Is it really yourself?'

'I am Mrs William Flynn,' the other woman replied. In her whisper voice.

Bríd made a clucking noise with her tongue. 'Muiris has taken Donal upriver to collect bait, but they will return soon. Would you have them see you like this?' She began to mop Mrs Flynn's wet face with her apron. 'Tomás, my comb is on the dresser. We need blankets too, you know where they are.'

'Tomflynn!' came a glad cry from overhead. Maura scrambled down the ladder from the loft. 'I was 'sleep,' she announced, 'but I'm 'wake now!' She flung herself at Tom and gave him a great hug. A moment later she was in Mrs Flynn's lap and hugging her too.

Soon the two Flynns were warm and dry and enjoying a hot meal. There was little chance for Bríd and Catherine to talk to each other. Maura monopolised the conversation with her customary babble about everything and nothing, punctuated with frequent hugs for the guests.

During a momentary lull Catherine managed to say, 'I was afraid you might hate me, Bríd.'

Before Bríd could answer the little girl exclaimed, 'We love you! We love you and Tomflynn lots!'

Muiris and Donal returned to find Bríd and Catherine sitting by the hearth, finishing the mending together. Tom was trying to teach Maura to count to ten. The cabin was filled with a warm glow which only partially came from the fire in the hearth.

An amazed Muiris paused in the doorway, hardly believing his eyes.

His wife glanced up. 'You're after letting the rain in, you foolish man. Be inside or be outside but don't be doing both at once.'

Catherine Flynn smiled at her brother. 'As you can see, Muiris, I am inside.'

* * *

Every member of the small community wanted to call on Catherine. Bríd decided against it. 'Caitríona is like a robin that lands on your outstretched hand. If people crowd around her she will be overwhelmed.'

Maura stationed herself at the door. Whenever someone

knocked the little girl opened the door just a crack and said, 'Tomflynn's mother is a robin. Don't 'whelm her.'

The day was far too short. When the light began to fade Catherine announced they must leave. Muiris urged her to spend the night but she declined. 'I have three girls waiting for me at home, and a household to run,' she reminded him.

'But you will come back?'

'It is not as far as I thought it was,' she said.

She and Tom were both tired. The rain had stopped but neither felt like talking. They saved their energy for the walk. Once Roaringwater House was in sight, however, Tom said, 'Did you think they hated you because of the money?'

'I suppose I did. It all happened so long ago and I was very young, but when I look back ...' She stopped walking. Tom waited.

'When I look back,' his mother said, 'I realise they did not hate me. We never really hate the people we love, even when they make us angry. I see now that my family was just disappointed in me. They thought I was turning my back on them.'

'And were you?'

'I was not! I was simply turning towards William. How strange,' she mused, 'that time has erased all that long-ago pain.'

'Footprints,' said Tom.

'What are you talking about?'

'Did you ever leave footprints on the beach, Mother, and come back later to find the sea had washed them away? It leaves the sand clean.'

Catherine Flynn smiled.

Tom's sisters were waiting eagerly to hear the details of the visit, but all Mrs Flynn said was, 'They were kind to us.' She went straight to her bed.

Tom answered their questions until he could not keep his eyes open any longer. Then he too retired. To the cave of the bed-closet.

On the following day Catherine Flynn had a talk with her children. 'When your father comes home again you are not to mention my brother or his family,' she said. 'Not a word about them, do you understand?'

Caroline immediately said, 'Why?'

'When William and I married there were certain problems ...'

'What sort of problems?' Virginia prompted.

'My people had once been very wealthy,' her mother explained, 'so William boasted of being related to the O'Flynns of Ardagh Castle, between Skibbereen and Baltimore. Like ourselves, they were a branch of the Corca Laoidhe.

'My father was still alive at the time. When he realised we were determined to marry, pride compelled him to give me a dowry appropriate to William's station. Shortly after the wedding I learned that William was merely a poor relation who had inherited a piece of land no one else wanted. I also discovered that the last of my family's fortune had gone into my dowry. A little honesty at the beginning would have prevented much resentment afterwards.'

'You would have married Father anyway,' guessed Elizabeth.

'Probably,' her mother admitted with a wry smile. 'We were very young. Unfortunately, as a result of some of the wild tales Seán told at our marriage feast, William thought the Ó Driscolls had a great hoard of hidden gold. He became obsessed with the idea. He convinced himself that my family had defrauded him and could have paid a much larger dowry. He forbade me to have anything more to do with them. To keep peace in the marriage, I agreed. If William knew Muiris had come here ...'

A look passed between Tom and his sisters. 'Father will not hear about it from us,' Elizabeth promised.

Elizabeth waited until she could catch Tom alone. 'Did you know anything about that?' she asked her brother.

'About what?'

'The tragic mistake both sides made, of course. Just imagine, Tom. Aside from Mother's dowry our parents started out with next nothing. They were very brave.'

Virginia joined them. Her face was flushed with excitement. 'You have seen how the Ó Driscolls live, Tom. Are they wealthy after all? Did they cheat Father?'

Tom gave his sister a withering look. 'You must be joking.'

'If they are wealthy,' said Virginia, 'I might be an heiress. Then I could go to Paris and study art.'

'And I would not have to marry Herbert Fox!' Elizabeth added.

* * *

Tom was now able to visit the narrow valley openly. As the days grew longer, he hurried with his lessons so there would be enough light left. His sisters pleaded to go with him but their mother continued to refuse. 'If all four of you go wandering along the coast someone will notice, and your father is bound to hear of it.'

Now it was Tom who was receiving special treatment. At first it was wonderful. Then he remembered how it felt to stand off to one side watching. He felt sorry for his sisters.

Elizabeth was fascinated by her newly-discovered relatives. 'We must begin calling on them soon,' she urged her mother. 'I am to be married this coming September. Ginny has made out all sorts of lists and we have to invite your family to the wedding. It would be a scandal to ignore them.'

It was the first time Elizabeth had demonstrated any interest in the upcoming wedding.

Herbert Fox, on the other hand, was showing no interest

at all. He paid no more calls on Elizabeth. For New Year he sent her a box of linen handkerchiefs.

'Cheap linen at that,' Missus remarked to Eithne. Elizabeth's marriage was a constant source of gossip below stairs. There was even a wager among the male servants. Only the head groom was betting that the wedding would take place.

The female servants were more hopeful. They would be disappointed if the excitement of another celebration was denied them.

Tom was disappointed when Muiris told him they were not doing any smuggling right now. 'Everything has a season,' he explained. 'Merchants are reluctant to send valuable cargos in the winter when they expect gales and ice.'

'But it's spring now,' Tom argued. 'Will we go out again soon?'

Muiris said, 'You are very keen, lad.'

'I like the sea. And the boats.'

'There are honest ways to enjoy both, Tomás. When you are a bit older—'

'When I am older my father wants me to be a soldier.'

'Is that what you want?'

'I just want to be a man, Muiris, and make my own decisions.'

'Men do not always get to make their own decisions. Sometimes life chooses for us. Do you think I wanted to be a smuggler? I used to compose poems. In our family Seán was the *seanachie* but I was the bard.' Muiris gave a careless shrug, dismissing all that could not be. 'If it is the sea and the boats you want, Tomás, I shall take you out myself and teach you to navigate in the bay.'

'Can I come too?' Donal pleaded.

Maura pounded her little fists against her father's hip. 'And me. And me!'

Muiris scooped her up, laughing. 'All of you, then. And if you turn us over and drown us, God 'a' mercy on us.'

On the first bright day when Tom had no lessons, Muiris and Seán took the three children out in a currach. The boys were given oars. Maura was perched in the prow and told to watch for sea-monsters.

'How will I know if I see one?'

Seán said seriously, 'A giant snake will come leaping out of the water with its nostrils breathing fire.'

Maura shook her head until her curls bounced. 'Will not. The water would put out the fire.'

'The only way to stay ahead of this girl is to get up yesterday,' said Muiris.

A dazzling spring day with a high wind blowing and feathery clouds streaming across the sky. Five people in a boat on the bay. Smiling and laughing. With not a care in the world.

CHAPTER TWENTY-THREE

RESCUE!

Simon paused at the doorway of the great hall. Catherine Flynn was sitting on a bench with her back to him. She appeared to be holding the harp. He took half a step sideways to get a better look. In his memory no one had ever touched the harp except for Missus, who dusted the carved frame occasionally.

Catherine brushed the fingers of one hand across the harp strings as lightly as if stroking them with a feather. Then she dropped her hand back into her lap. 'Come in, Simon,' she said without looking around. 'I shall not play, I've quite forgotten how.'

'No one forgets how to make music,' he said.

'I have forgotten too many things. Was there any post for us in the village?'

He held out the letter. 'This arrived this morning.'

'Thank you, Simon.' She carried the letter upstairs to her bed-chamber, broke the wax seal and opened the envelope.

My dearest Kate,

I am writing this letter on a rainy morning in late April. It is my last deed before leaving Ireland. The Earl of Strafford has raised a private army of 8000 foot soldiers and 1000 cavalry, including my own company. The troops are massed on the Dublin docks, waiting to board ship. As soon as I post this letter I shall join them. We depart for Scotland today. You should see how splendid we look! The wild Scots cannot possibly stand against us.

I may not have the opportunity to write again until we have won a victory or two, but do not worry about me. Since meeting Robert Boyle things have turned around for me. That young man proved to be my good luck charm. Perhaps we underestimate our children.

Robert is estranged from his father, which is a loss to both of them. A man's sons are his bridge to the future. I may have been too harsh with my own son. Just as Robert Boyle is not to blame for the deeds of his father, Tom is not to blame for what happened all these years ago. When I return I shall be in a position to make amends to him.

We have high hopes for this undertaking. Once the rebellion is put down, we expect the king to follow royal custom

and reward his officers with grants of prime land. You will
be able to leave that inadequate house, Kate. I shall give you
a home more worthy of you, perhaps a castle in Scotland. ...

Catherine Flynn put down the letter. 'What does he
mean by "inadequate"?' she asked the walls of her chamber. The proportions of the room were pleasing to her eyes.
In summer the great windows caught the morning light. In
winter the fireplace filled the chamber with a golden glow.
And the thick walls made sure it was always quiet. When she
was a child she had grown so tired of the sound of the sea.
William had carefully placed their house so she would not
have to hear that endless, exhausting voice.

Her home was not a mansion, though her husband per-
sisted in calling it one. It was just a draughty country house,
better than some but plainer than most. Catherine Flynn
did not want a mansion, and certainly not a castle. Her heart
was cemented into the rubblestone walls of Roaringwater
House.

Now William proposed to transplant her like the English
rose bushes he insisted on buying every year. Uprooted from
their native earth and sent across the sea to foreign soil, they
always died.

She picked up the letter again.

I have always shielded you from financial concerns, but there is something I must tell you. As you know, for a number of years I have been doing business with Herbert Fox. That is over now. We quarrelled on the day I sailed from Cobh. Fox demanded I give Elizabeth's dowry to him immediately. I succeeded in putting him off, but sooner rather than later he will repeat his demand. He may even ask for more.

The man is a total scoundrel, Kate, and greedy to a fault. I have decided that I do not want my daughter to marry him. In anticipation of our success in Scotland I have concluded new monetary arrangements. Therefore I no longer need Herbert Fox. I insist that Elizabeth break off the engagement.

I hope the girl will not be too upset. You must assure her that, as always, her father knows best.

* * *

Bright clear sunlight glittered on Roaringwater Bay. The waves appeared to be crested with diamonds. For a while Muiris talked about tides and currents and navigation, but it was too much information for Tom to take in at one time. He listened as hard as he could – until he began to yawn. The sun was very warm.

Muiris noticed the yawn. Turning towards Seán, he began a teasing banter. Soon they were exchanging the fond insults of brothers.

How lucky I am, Tom thought drowsily. I have two families, with an almost brother and an almost baby sister.

'Have you seen any sea-monsters yet?' he called to Maura.

'Not yet, Tomflynn. Can we eat monsters?'

'I don't think so. Why, are you hungry?'

She patted her tummy. 'Always hungry.'

Muiris said, 'Bríd packed some food for us. We can go ashore on one of the islands and eat.'

'Now?'

'Not now, Maura,' her father replied. 'You have to find a monster first.' He winked at Tom, who winked back.

Maura squinted at the water. After a few minutes she announced, 'I see one! Can we eat now?'

'Where is it?'

'Over there.' She pointed. 'No, over there!' She pointed in a different direction.

'Keep looking,' Seán said with a grin.

The sun was warm, the wind was gentle. The oars sang *tloc swoosh, tloc swoosh, tloc swoosh*. Tom felt himself growing sleepy. Seán and Muiris began arguing over which one of them was ... was ...

'Monster!' announced Maura. She leaned far out, pointing again. This time nobody looked.

So nobody saw the large black object just below the surface until the boat struck the rock.

The jolt threw Maura from the currach.

The little girl's terrified scream woke Tom. By the time he realised what was happening Donal had leapt to his feet and lunged forward, vainly trying to catch his sister. In his anxiety Donal lost his balance. And followed her into the sea.

The water closed over them both.

Muiris cried in horror, 'They can't swim!'

None of their family could. As Séamus had once explained to Tom, 'Men who make their living on the sea do not want to be able to swim. If a man loses his ship he could spend terrified hours struggling in the water, only to drown in the end. Better to drown straight away and be done.'

Tom had not admitted to Séamus that he could swim. He wanted to be like the rest of them. Without allowing himself time to think, he held his breath and jumped overboard.

He sank like a stone.

Down he plummeted, farther down than he had expected. This was not the shallow water beyond the beach. This was the deep bay. Down, down he went into the dark, until he heard a roaring in his ears. Trying not to panic, he began moving his arms and legs. He could not paddle the way he did on the surface. He was not even sure where the surface was. Which way was up?

His toes tried in vain to touch the bottom.

There was no bottom!

He was too frightened to think of a prayer. God, he said in his head. The one word. God. In the dark and the cold.

Then he realised he was rising. Up and up, until he popped onto the surface like a cork from a bottle.

One quick gasp of air and Tom started down again. This time he reached forward with his arms and kicked strongly with his legs, taking control.

A solid body bumped against his and glanced off. Maura's sea monster! He had not realised his eyes were closed until he opened them. It was Maura herself, drifting away from him. He reached for the little girl but she was gone before he could catch her.

Tom propelled himself to the surface long enough to take another gulp of air, then went down after her.

Her skirt ballooned upwards as she sank. He caught hold of it and hung on with all his strength, dragging her towards him. When he could get an arm around the child's waist he began to fight his way back to the surface. It was the hardest thing he had ever done. His lungs were near to bursting. Maura was limp. He did not know if she was alive or dead.

They came up not far from the currach. Muiris was in the water by then, holding onto an oar which Seán was extending from the boat.

'Tomás!' Seán shouted. 'This way!'

Tom tried to swim to Muiris. With only one arm free it

was difficult. Maura was a dead weight, further slowing his progress. But he could never turn her loose. He held her tight against his body. Her head was tucked beneath his chin. He was Tomflynn and she was his little sister and he would not let her go. Not even to save himself.

Seán and Muiris were both shouting to him now. He dare not answer. If he swallowed water he might drown. Then Maura would surely drown – if she was not dead already. No! Tom refused to accept that possibility. Yet he could feel a cramp beginning in one of his legs. A cramp now could prove fatal.

Muiris stretched his arm as far as he could; stretched so desperately he thought his joints would pull apart. Stretched still farther. Saw Tom's white face grimace with pain as the boy struggled to reach him. Glimpsed the top of Maura's head, her dark curls plastered to her skull. Her dear, dark curls ...

One more mighty effort beyond human strength ... and Muiris closed his hand around Tom's wrist.

CHAPTER TWENTY-FOUR

INTO THE DEPTHS

Seán braced himself in the currach to hold the oar steady while Muiris drew Tom and Maura to the side of the boat. 'All right, Tomás,' Muiris said hoarsely. 'I can take her now.' He reached for his daughter but Tom could not release her. His arm was locked in place around the little girl.

The two men – one in the water and one in the boat – had to lift Tom and Maura over the side together.

Gasping for breath, Tom slumped in the bottom of the currach while Maura's father and uncle bent over her. Muiris began talking in Irish to the little girl. Urging her to live. To Tom's relief, he heard her cough and splutter. She called in a weak voice for Donal.

Muiris looked over his shoulder. His eyes met Tom's.

This time Tom knew what to expect. Yet he went over the side anyway, back into the sea.

'Why did you let him do that!' Seán cried accusingly.

'How could I stop him?'

'How could you not, *amadán*? If Cait's son dies trying to

save yours she will never forgive any of us.'

The two men glared at each other across the body of the little girl who was just coming back to life. Then they turned to look at the sea. The water was dark and choppy, a constantly moving seascape. Somewhere down there Tom had disappeared as surely as if the bay had swallowed him.

Muiris gave a single moan of despair. His expression quickly changed to determination. 'They are still here, Seán, they have to be, and we can find them. Take up your oars; hurry!'

Tom was unaware of what was happening on the surface. He had returned to a hostile world where he knew he could not survive for long. He must make every moment count. He peered into the watery gloom, looking for Donal.

When Maura fell from the prow she had gone straight down. Donal had fallen from the middle of the boat – how much difference would that make? The bay was huge, and the currents which Muiris had been describing earlier were strong. Donal might be anywhere by now. The only thing to do was keep searching for him as long as he could.

Which would not be long. Tom's strength was almost gone.

He swam to the surface to take one more breath of air. When his head cleared the water he tossed the hair out of his eyes. They were stinging painfully from the salt. He could hardly see. There was a sort of blob which might be the boat, he could not tell. He thought he heard shouting again, but over the noise of the wind and the waves he could not be sure.

Tom took a big gulp of air and went back down. One more time, he told himself. I can do this one more time.

He went down as far as he dared, until there was just enough air left in his lungs to get him back to the surface.

A hand grabbed his ankle.

Instinctively he tried to kick free.

Then he realised it must be Donal. He twisted, reached down, found the arm that was attached to the hand, and pulled. Donal rose in the water beside him. The other boy's eyes were open. His face was contorted into a grimace of terror.

Tom pointed upward. He could not tell if Donal understood, but he started swimming in that direction. He meant to carry his friend with him. Donal responded by trying to climb him like a tree, threatening in his panic to drag them both down.

After the day they first met, Tom had never matched his strength against Donal's. Now he must.

'I tell you I saw Donal!' Seán was shouting. 'Just over there, Muiris! He came up for a moment and vanished again. But they come up three times, do they not? Three times?'

'Maybe he had come up twice already and we were looking the other way. What about Tomás?'

'I don't see anyone now,' said Seán. 'They're gone. But we

have to ... we must ...'

'We must,' echoed Muiris, his heart breaking. He knew what neither of them could say. Must search the coastline for the bodies and pray they eventually came ashore.

Something struck the bottom of the currach.

Seán swore at the rock that had caused this tragedy.

'That did not feel like a rock,' Muiris told him.

The bump came again. 'More like a dolphin ...' Muiris looked over the side. 'Seán, quick! Help me!'

Together the brothers pulled an exhausted, watersoaked boy out of the water.

And then another one.

* * *

The little island with its crown of trees was the most beautiful sight Tom had ever seen. By the time they beached the currach he had recovered enough to help Donal ashore. Muiris carried Maura in his arms.

As soon as they were on dry land the little girl said, 'Can we eat now?'

Seán's laughter was almost hysterical with relief. 'Bless the child, I'll find an ox and slaughter and butcher it myself.'

'Don't like ox meat,' Maura declared. 'Like bread and buttermilk.'

They ate while sun and wind dried their clothes. Tom discovered he was ravenous. 'I don't want anything wet,' Donal said, ignoring the buttermilk. But he consumed a huge amount of bread and cheese. Only Muiris had no appetite. When Seán offered him food he refused. 'I could have lost all of you,' he said to the three children.

'But you didn't,' Tom pointed out. 'Have some cheese.'

'I owe you a greater debt than I can ever repay, Tomás.'

'You don't owe me anything. Just take me smuggling with you the next time you go.'

Before Muiris could reply Donal said, 'I didn't know you could swim.'

'I taught myself last summer. I practised in the cove on days when you didn't come.'

'But why?'

'Because the water was there.' Even as Tom said the words, he knew it was no answer. Yet it was the only answer he could give. Why does anyone do anything?

He turned back to Muiris. 'Will you take me smuggling the next time you go?'

The man shook his head. 'I cannot, Tomás. Smuggling is not something we did for pleasure, and I pray we never have to do it again. But even if we were going tomorrow I would not bring you. Letting you join us was an act of revenge on my part. Now that I have seen my sister again, I regret it.'

Tom frowned. 'I don't understand.'

'I took you to get even with your father. It was my revenge

for his taking Caitríona from us.'

Seán said, 'You never told me that.'

'I am the chief,' Muiris reminded him. 'I do not tell you everything.'

Tom could not help laughing. 'You wanted revenge against my father, Muiris. So did I! I wanted to join the smugglers to help make a fool of my father.'

'Now I do not understand,' said Muiris.

Donal spoke up. 'I think I do. I saw a Persian rug in your house, Tomás. For several months we had that rug stored in the cave. I know it's the same one, because I used to unroll it to look at the horses and peacocks.'

Tom was nodding. 'I suspect Father's been buying smuggled goods for years without knowing it.'

Muiris raised one eyebrow. 'Are you sure he did not know?'

CHAPTER TWENTY-FIVE

THE BATTLEFIELD

lizabeth composed a letter to Herbert Fox, breaking off their engagement. She did not use the elaborate, flowery language in which she had been schooled, the proper language for a lady's correspondence. She used the bare minimum of words. She did not want to give him anything more.

Dear Mr Fox,

With my father's approval I wish to end our betrothal. I shall not marry you.

Sincerely, Miss Elizabeth Flynn.

She hoped that would be the end of it.

The brief, bright summer of 1640 arrived overnight in Roaringwater Bay. One day was cold and overcast. The following day was radiant, with a warm wind blowing from the south and every leaf a-shimmer.

Mr Beasley had packed up and departed the scene, leaving

Tom free to spend as much time as he liked with his uncle's family. At first he went almost every day. There was always work he could help with, and he loved fishing. The currachs did not go far out in the bay, however. They stayed close to home, fishing in shallow water.

Maura was not allowed anywhere near them.

By July, Tom's visits to the valley became less frequent. There he was treated as a hero now, which made him uncomfortable. At Roaringwater House he was just Tom. His mother still tried to baby him, his sisters' conversations still bored him, and when he thought about his father he still had mixed feelings.

On the first of August Catherine Flynn wrote a long letter to her husband and sent it to him in care of the Dublin post office. She had been writing a similar letter every fortnight since his departure for Scotland.

She had yet to receive a reply.

* * *

William Flynn grunted with the effort of pulling off his heavy boots.

'This was not a good day, Captain Flynn,' said the man slumped beside him in the heather.

'No, it was not,' Flynn agreed. 'We have not had many good days since we arrived in this godforsaken country, Major. I do not mind telling you, I expected something rather different.'

'As did I,' said his companion. 'When I received my commission I thought it would include ... shall we say ... spoils of war?'

Flynn lifted his head to look at the other man. Although they were in the uplands, which were supposed to be cool, the August sun was fierce. Sweat was rolling down the major's forehead. He was dressed in a maroon-coloured coat over which he wore breast and back plates formed from sheet iron. His polished iron helmet shimmered in the heat. He looked like a man being roasted alive.

Flynn had taken off his helmet but his woollen coat was bad enough. He was thankful he had not been able to purchase body armour.

Could not purchase anything now anyway. Last coin spent. Pockets full of lint. Sounds like a poem, he thought. Do poets ever write about the losing side?

'Spoils of war,' he said aloud. 'A polite term for plunder. I suppose there will be no plunder now.'

'I'm afraid not,' the major confirmed. 'No reward of any kind. Not even the thanks of the Lord Lieutenant.' He sounded bitter.

At the mention of Thomas Wentworth, Flynn sat up. 'Where is Strafford?'

'The last I heard of him, he and the king together were trying to raise funds to support the war. They got a trickle of money but it never reached us. For all I know Strafford's still in London. He is too clever to share our defeat.'

Flynn slumped back into the heather. 'One pitiful skirmish, and then goodbye. We'll be lucky to get back to Ireland with our lives.' He picked up his badly dented helmet and held it towards the major. 'See that? Grazed by a Scottish musket ball. Should have taken my head off.'

'Where's that bold horse of yours?'

'He was too bold,' said Flynn. 'He had no stomach for cowards. When our troops panicked at the first cannonade he threw me off in disgust and left the field. Where's yours?'

'Killed under me. I never had a horse die under me before. It is a rotten experience, I can tell you. He would have made a fine hunter when this was over.'

'How are we supposed to replace them?' Flynn wondered. 'We are a hundred miles from anywhere and my feet are too swollen to go back into my boots.'

'You still have your pistol, Captain?'

'I do. Lost the sword somewhere, but I still have this.' Flynn drew a wheel-lock pistol from his belt.

'Use it to relieve some other poor sod of his mount,' the major advised. 'That is what I mean to do. Then ride like the devil for the nearest port and hope to take a ship for Ireland before they catch us.'

'Before who catches us?'

'The world and his wife,' said the major.

* * *

Summer was over. The slanting light of autumn lay across the bay. On a September day when the wind was in the east and the sea was the colour of lead, Herbert Fox unexpectedly appeared at Roaringwater House. Simon opened the door for him and showed him inside. Then he went to tell Mrs Flynn.

She was startled. 'Why is that man here, Simon?'

'He did not tell me, madam. He only said he wants to see you.'

'Bring him to me in the hall, then, but stay within earshot. There might be an unpleasant scene.'

Mrs Flynn held her head high and her back straight, though her hands were trembling. She hid them in the folds of her skirt as she faced the visitor. To her surprise he seemed to be in a good mood. He offered a courteous little bow and several minutes' worth of pleasant conversation before coming to the point.

'As you know,' said Fox, 'I have released your daughter from our engagement. I cannot marry a woman who no longer desires to be my wife. I would never do anything against a lady's wishes. I like the ladies.' He smiled, revealing stained yellow teeth. 'In fact, I am here today to do a favour for another lady – yourself, dear Mrs Flynn.'

She raised her eyebrows politely. 'What sort of favour?'

'In this backwater you must be unaware of what happens in the larger world. Knowing your husband as I do, I doubt he tells you anything of importance.'

'Is William all right?'

'Calm yourself, dear lady. I am not bringing bad news, at least not about your husband. But the campaign he joined has gone very wrong.' Fox showed still more teeth. He was enjoying this.

Mrs Flynn repressed a shudder.

'Allow me to explain,' Fox said. 'Going to war is an expensive business. Instead of raising sufficient money for the king's campaign against the Scots, the English parliament turned against the king. Meanwhile Strafford's attempt to raise money through the Irish parliament met with little success. Promises were made. But that is as far as it went.

'In May the king dissolved the English parliament. Since then everything has changed. Now the question is who really holds the power in England: the monarch or the parliament? This may be the end for the king. There are very clever men against him.'

'Surely no one would harm the king!'

'One would hope not, dear lady. However, situations change. In August a Scottish army crossed the border into England to fight the king. They chose their time well. Strafford's troops had not yet been fully deployed and the English soldiers were untrained and lacked discipline. The king's forces panicked before a cannonade at Newburg. The Scots gained a nearly bloodless victory that day.

'The king is deeply upset. He does not accept any blame, of course; kings never do. The blame is being shifted to the shoulders of the Earl of Strafford. Thomas Wentworth will be the scapegoat for everything that goes wrong. Richard Boyle and his friends are whipping up a great wave of resentment against him. At the first sitting of the new parliament, Strafford's enemies intend to accuse him of invading crown territory with a private army for his personal gain.'

Mrs Flynn opened her eyes very wide. 'But that is not true.'

Fox replied in the voice he would use for speaking to a child. 'The truth, dear lady, is whatever the men in power say it is.'

'I do not believe you!'

'You should; it is a valuable lesson to learn. And one more thing you should know. Thomas Wentworth will be tried for treason. The king will throw him to the wolves to draw attention away from his own failures.'

Catherine Flynn was on the verge of tears. 'How can you possibly know all these terrible things?'

'I make it my business to know them. Knowledge is power, dear lady. I have it. Your husband does not.'

'William is still alive, then?'

'I am told that he is, and I have reliable informants. A man with enough ships has ears everywhere.'

Catherine Flynn sat very still. Then she licked her dry lips. 'Simon?' she called. 'Tell Missus to prepare a bedroom for our guest, and be sure that his horse is stabled and fed.' With an effort, she arranged her features into a pleasant expression. 'You will be joining us for dinner, Mr Fox?'

His eyes glinted. 'Of course.'

Elizabeth was horrified. 'I will not sit at table with that man! Mother cannot ask it of me. Why is he here, Tom?'

'Mr Fox brought news for Mother.'

'On the very day we were supposed to be married? Herbert Fox has another reason for coming here, you can count on it. Make him go away, Tom. You saved two children from drowning. Surely you can get rid of one ugly old man.'

CHAPTER TWENTY-SIX

A DIFFERENT KIND OF STORM

In support of their sister, Virginia and Caroline also failed to appear for dinner. Tom found himself sitting on one side of the table with Herbert Fox on the other, and Mrs Flynn at the end. There was not much conversation. Plates and cutlery made a loud clatter in the quiet room.

When Tom asked him to pass the butter, Mr Fox was annoyed because the boy said 'Please', and then 'Thank you'.

Mrs Flynn put down her three-tined fork and cleared her throat. 'Mr Fox, you say my husband is alive. Will he be home soon?'

Tom looked up.

'I think he will,' Fox replied. 'I hear that Strafford's men fled from their defeat like rats from a sinking ship.'

Tom said angrily, 'My father never fled from anything. I resent a fox calling him a rat.'

'Tom!' Mrs Flynn exclaimed. 'You must apologise to our guest.'

'I'm not the one who owes an apology.'

'*Tom*,' she said again.

He relented. He could not humiliate his mother. 'I apologise,' he muttered. 'May I be excused now?'

Mrs Flynn nodded.

He pushed back his chair and stood up. As he crossed the room he could feel Herbert Fox's eyes boring into his back.

Virginia and Elizabeth were lying in wait for Tom outside the door. 'We heard everything,' Virginia said. 'Imagine that wretched man calling Father a rat!'

'Do something about him, Tom,' Elizabeth pleaded again.

He drew a deep breath. *Roaring at the top of his lungs, courageous General Thomas Flynn rushed back into the room: Leave this house at once, Mr Fox, and never darken our doorway again!* Tom slowly exhaled. 'He would only laugh at me, Lizzie. Boys don't give orders to men.'

'Sugar and cream!' swore Virginia. 'I'm really disappointed in you!'

In the morning Herbert Fox enjoyed a lavish breakfast, helping himself to double portions of everything. Tom expected the man would depart soon afterwards. He went to the stable himself to have Fox's horse made ready.

Instead Fox examined William Flynn's collection of books, selected one with a lot of illustrations, and sat down in the hall to look at them.

By evening he was still there.

It was not polite to ask a guest when he was going to leave. Yet the visitor's continued presence in the house was unsettling. 'I think Mother's afraid of him,' Caroline said.

Virginia disagreed. 'Father and Mr Fox do business together, don't they, Lizzie? Mother's only being nice to him on that account.'

'She's being nice to him because he has information about Father,' Tom said.

'This is not about business or Father,' Elizabeth stated with conviction. She dropped her voice to a whisper. 'Herbert Fox is a horrid man. Believe me when I tell you: he's here to take revenge because I hurt his pride. He might do anything.'

Tears welled in Caroline's eyes. 'Oh how I wish Father were here!'

* * *

The following morning Fox was the first person down for breakfast.

Foregoing his own meal, Tom headed for the narrow valley.

Muiris and his brothers had gone hunting. Donal was there, however. He was stretching a wet cowhide between pegs driven into the earth. 'I'm going to make a coracle,' he told Tom. 'It's time I had my own boat.'

Tom tried to raise one eyebrow the way Muiris did. It was not a success. He merely twitched his forehead. 'Don't you think you should learn to swim first, Donal?'

Donal gave a careless shrug. 'There's plenty of time for that. Let's go cut willow branches for the framework of the boat.'

Tom joined his friend, though he could not concentrate on the task. His thoughts kept returning to Roaringwater House. Maura soon appeared to make suggestions of her own for the project. Donal was amused and exasperated by turns, but even the little girl's antics could not lift Tom's spirits.

At midday Bríd prepared a meal of hot bread and hotter soup. When Tom tried to eat, the shadow of Herbert Fox looked over his shoulder. He pushed the bowl away with an apology. 'I think I had too much breakfast.'

Without waiting for Muiris to return, Tom set off for home. He was trying to convince himself that Herbert Fox had gone. Surely the man knew he was not wanted. As Tom passed the stables he paused to look in the boxes. Fox's horse was still there, munching corn. His saddle and bridle had been cleaned and hung up for another day.

Tom entered the house with dragging feet. Smoking a foul-smelling pipe, the uninvited guest was occupying Mr Flynn's favourite chair in the great hall. Mrs Flynn and her daughters were at the other end of the room. Tom thought they looked like sheep waiting to be shorn.

Fox greeted the boy with another of his yellow smiles. 'Ah, Tom! Do join us. I was just telling these dear ladies how much I appreciate their hospitality. I have decided to stay on for a while, so I can be on hand to welcome your dear father when he returns home. We have a little business to discuss. It will be the perfect opportunity.'

Tom shot a glance at his mother. She would not meet his eyes.

Elizabeth looked furious.

Tom went to his room and slammed the door.

In the morning Herbert Fox was again the first person at the breakfast table. He tried to get Mrs Flynn to call him 'Bertie' and insisted on calling her Catherine.

None of the servants liked the man. 'He is far too full of himself,' was Eithne's verdict. 'He's the wind in his own sails,' declared Simon, who neglected to polish his boots. Missus did not shake out his featherbed. Cook put too much salt in his food. Stable boy and scullery maid alike insulted him behind his back.

Tom's mother continued to address him as Mr Fox.

After his visit to the valley Tom stayed close to home. A storm was gathering over Roaringwater House. Light fading, pressure building. Not the kind of storm that could be cleared away by a clap of thunder. This storm was like a crouching animal. Tom could sense it in the hall and on the stairs, at the dining table and even in his bed-chamber. When

CHAPTER TWENTY-SEVEN

TOM GETS SOME ANSWERS

Roaringwater House became an armed camp. Tom and his sisters were on one side, Herbert Fox on the other. When Fox occupied the great hall as if it were his own, the younger Flynns were careful to be elsewhere. They insisted on taking their meals after Fox had eaten. This made extra work for Cook, who grumbled to her mistress. All Mrs Flynn said was, 'Leave them be, Cook.'

Catherine Flynn was caught in the middle of the silent war. The drawn look returned to her face and her appetite failed – in spite of Cook's best efforts with the spices.

Mr Fox had a comment, however. Although his own food was over-salted, he claimed, 'I have never tasted better food. I could eat like this for the rest of my life.'

'When Father comes home he'll sort that man out,' Virginia predicted.

Elizabeth was not so sure. 'Herbert Fox would not be

waiting for Father if he were afraid of him.'

* * *

The William Flynn who returned to Roaringwater House in the autumn was very different from the William Flynn who had left in the spring. Gone was the jaunty confidence. Gone too were the men who had followed him. He was alone.

He drew rein on the hired horse he was riding, and sat staring at the house. It looked just as he remembered. Yet what had been beautiful to him once was ugly now. A dream gone sour.

Catherine. Oh, my Kate.

He heaved a sigh and kicked the weary horse. 'Walk on, you poor brute,' he said. 'We may end up in the knacker's yard together.'

William Flynn did not enter his front door, but rode around to the stable yard. 'Give this beast a good meal,' he told the groom. 'I don't want to have to pay for him if he dies. What's that bay horse doing in the best loose box?'

'He belongs to your guest,' the groom said.

'What guest?'

'Miss Elizabeth's fiancé.'

'Her what? Are you certain?'

'I am of course. He's been here for weeks.'

William Flynn ran into the house. A score of possibilities,

all of them bad, were racing through his mind.

When he opened the door of the great hall he saw his wife and Herbert Fox on opposite sides of the fireplace. Mrs Flynn sat stiffly erect on a padded stool, trying to hide behind her wooden embroidery frame. Mr Fox slouched in William Flynn's favourite chair with his legs stretched out in front of him. 'Ah, William!' he said without bothering to get to his feet. He might have been addressing a servant. 'You've returned at last, I see. Did you have a pleasant time in England?'

'Why are you here?'

'Is that any way to greet an old friend who is paying a social call on your family? I fear I have been neglecting them – like you have been neglecting your property. Take that Persian rug for example.' Fox nodded towards the item in question. 'A work of art, really. Yet it is damaged.'

Flynn tried to hold his temper. 'I did not cause the damage. You did it yourself on the night of the betrothal party.'

Fox smiled his ugly smile. 'So I did. When I saw the rug that evening I realised you had been holding out on me, and I was angry. I am over it now. I am not one to carry a grudge – not if I can find a way to even the score.' The smile grew wider. 'You should congratulate me on my good fortune, William. Or should I say on my excellent business sense? While you were away I made a clever investment. I bought up a mortgage from one of Richard Boyle's moneylenders.'

'Eh?'

'You heard me. I bought a mortgage on a piece of property which I have had my eye on for some time. Several years, in fact. The house is undistinguished in my opinion, and the land is far removed from any real civilisation. But since the place overlooks Roaringwater Bay it is perfectly suited to my purpose. You understand why, William,' he said meaningfully.

The colour drained from Flynn's face. He cast a despairing glance at his wife, who had risen to her feet. 'What have you told my family, Herbert?'

'Nothing, yet. Why don't we call the children in here and get this over with? Or perhaps you would prefer to explain to them and your wife by yourself? I can be generous, you see, when I hold a winning hand. I shall leave you alone for a while.' Fox stood up and sauntered from the hall. Just outside the door he paused and shouted, 'Come down, children! Your dear father is home and has news for you.'

Tom was the first into the hall. His sisters pushed past him and ran to their father. He hugged each of the girls in turn, without really looking at them, then held out his hand to his wife. 'You had best sit down again, Kate. There is something I must tell you.'

Flynn had the haunted expression of a man on his way to the gallows.

'When I left here last spring I fully expected to be part

of a victorious army,' he said. 'Because I thought I could pay it back, I borrowed money in Dublin. Some of it went to equip myself and my company. I was sure the Lord Lieutenant would reimburse me.' Flynn tried to sound reassuring. 'Everyone was so certain ...' His courage failed him. 'I signed a promissory note, Kate,' he admitted in an embarrassed voice. 'A mortgage on Roaringwater House. The man who loaned me the money was one of Boyle's moneylenders.'

Suddenly his wife understood. 'Oh, William!' She swayed on her chair. 'You signed our home away?'

In one long stride Flynn had his arms around her. Tom ran toward them but his father put out a hand to stop him. 'Stand back, boy.'

'I won't! She's my mother.'

'And my wife. I want to protect her as much as you do.'

'Liar!' Tom exploded. 'I know what a mortgage is. It means Herbert Fox owns this house now. How could you risk Mother's home just so you could ride around on a new horse and wear plumes in your hat?' Tom was afraid if he said anything more he would either cry or hit his father. He broke off speaking and ran from the room.

'Go after him, William,' his mother urged.

'Why should I? Did you hear what he called me? I don't have to take that from—'

'Go after him,' said Catherine. Her voice was no longer soft.

Flynn caught up with Tom in the stable yard. When he shouted 'Boy!', Tom stopped. Turned. Faced his father.

I will not run any more. I will not be afraid any longer.

Carrying a pitchfork, the groom emerged from one of the loose boxes. 'Is there trouble?' he asked anxiously.

Flynn waved him away. 'Leave us,' he ordered.

'Now listen to me, boy,' he said to Tom. 'You have this all wrong, you do not understand the situation.'

Colour rose in Tom's cheeks. 'Why should I believe anything you say? You hate me,' he accused. 'You've always hated me.'

His father looked surprised. 'I never hated you. I may not have expressed affection for you, but that is not my way.'

'You are affectionate enough to my sisters,' Tom said.

'It is different with them.'

'How? How is it different, Father?'

The man balled his fists. 'You have no right to question me, boy.'

Tom stood his ground. 'I believe I do. I've been the man of the family while you were away, and I've been learning things I never knew before. Now I want to hear the truth from you.'

'I have always been honest with you,' said his father.

'If that's true, answer this: why do you hate me?'

William Flynn relaxed his fists. 'I doubt if you could understand.'

'Try me,' Tom urged.

The man gathered his thoughts. Things were happening too fast. He had lost the ability to resist. He said tentatively, 'We must go back a few years ... '

'I'm listening.'

'Your mother was lovely in her youth,' Flynn recalled. 'The loveliest creature I ever saw.' A light came into his eyes. 'Although her family was notorious throughout the region, she had many suitors. I was a youngest son and could not expect much of an inheritance – aside from a useless bit of land on Roaringwater Bay. But I had enough brains to court and win the woman I wanted.

'I persuaded Catherine's father to settle a substantial dowry on her. After we married she gave me three daughters in succession. With each one my wife grew more beautiful. By the time you were on the way she was breathtaking.' Flynn swallowed hard.

'Using her dowry,' he went on, 'I hired the architect who had built Palace Anne at Ballineen. I instructed him to create a suitable setting for my wife. Once we had a big house, I set out to make important friends. My ultimate plan was to gain a seat in the Irish Parliament. It was to be my tribute to Catherine and erase the taint of her heritage. Instead of shame, she would feel only pride.

'You came along when I had almost given up hope of having a son. You were to be the crown on my happiness.

Alas, things did not go well. You were a large baby, and your mother was damaged giving birth to you. She became the frail, faded woman she is today.' Flynn's voice sank. 'I blamed you for costing me the wife I loved. I have never known how to treat you, boy.'

'Tom.'

'Eh?'

'My name is Tom.'

William Flynn gave his son a long look. He remembered Robert Boyle's words: *I envy him, having the love of a father.* 'Tom,' he said at last.

The person standing in front of the boy was not the William Flynn he had known all his life. Tom realised that his father was a broken man.

'Are we really going to lose the house?' Tom asked.

His father seemed to shrink inside his clothes. 'And the land,' he admitted. 'Yes, I am afraid we are. We cannot expect pity from Herbert Fox. He has always been merciless to those in his power.'

Random threads were coming together in Tom's mind, forming a pattern, like that in the Persian rug. 'Did Mr Fox force you to give him Elizabeth?'

'He ... persuaded me,' said Flynn. 'Herbert can be very persuasive. You see, he knows certain damaging things about me. He hinted that he would tell my wife unless I agreed to the match. So I did. You must understand, I was not being totally selfish. I truly believed he would take care of Elizabeth. In the beginning he gave a good imitation of being fond of her. Now I see why he really wanted her.

'You are still very young, Tom. If anything happened to me, no one would be surprised if my son-in-law took over the management of my property for the sake of my family. It is not uncommon.' Flynn paused. Shook himself, like someone trying to throw off a nightmare. 'But I made it even easier for him. Through my own foolishness, I handed him everything on a plate.'

Tom said, 'What damaging things does he know about you?'

His father shifted his feet. Would not meet his son's eyes. 'The details of my business.'

When Tom spoke again it was with calm authority, the voice of command. 'And just what business is that, Father? You had best tell me.'

The answer came out of the man's mouth like teeth being pulled. 'Herbert ... acquires ... various expensive items from abroad. Items that are in much demand here among the propertied classes. He does this in a way which means he pays no taxes on them. He's very clever, you see. I mean ... I used to think he was very clever. For years I have been selling the merchandise for him in Dublin.'

The pattern was clear now. Tom said, 'But you secretly kept some of the things for yourself. Like the Persian rug.'

'Shrewd guess,' said his father.

'I'm not guessing.'

'All right, so I kept some choice items. I was entitled to take them. Herbert never did give me my fair share of the profits, and I wanted fine things for your mother.'

'What would happen if the king's agents found out about this business of yours?'

'I would be thrown into prison,' Flynn said bleakly.

'And Mr Fox with you?'

'Herbert knows many men in government. Greedy men like himself. He has built up a sizeable fortune over the years, and would be able to buy his way out of trouble. I am not in the same privileged position.' Flynn slumped onto the mounting block and buried his face in his hands. 'I am defeated, Tom,' he moaned. 'Step by step, I have brought disaster on us all. How can you ever forgive me?'

CHAPTER TWENTY-EIGHT

THE CHILDREN TAKE ACTION

William Flynn went to bed drunk. And woke up the following morning wishing he were still drunk. Knowing Herbert Fox remained in his house. Gloating. Tormenting the women with his presence.

'You might as well pack your personal things when I go to Cork to have the new title drawn up,' Fox had told them last night. 'I shall not leave until the weekend, to give me adequate time to survey my new property with William as my guide. You can go to Cork with me if you like, Elizabeth. We can be married there.'

In floods of tears, Elizabeth had fled to her room.

Fox laughed.

* * *

Donal was fishing from his little coracle when he heard a shout from the cliffs. Looking up, he saw Tom waving to him. He rowed toward the shingle beach.

Tom hurried down the hidden path to join him. 'I'm so glad you're here!' he told his friend. 'I took a chance you might be.'

Donal noticed his flushed face. 'What's wrong, Tomás?'

The words burst out of him. 'A man is taking our house and land.'

Donal thought it was a joke. He laughed. 'Taking it where?'

'He's trying to claim ownership of it,' Tom amended. 'But I'm not going to let him. Let's go find Muiris. I'll explain to you on the way.'

As they were rowing into the marshy river mouth Donal said, 'I never heard of a mortgage before. Are you sure you have it right? Someone else can actually own what is yours?'

'I don't understand it completely myself,' Tom replied. With his oar he pushed the coracle away from a clump of willows. 'I wish I had paid more attention when Mr Beasley was talking about business and keeping accounts. I suspect Muiris will know what a mortgage is, though. He knows about a lot of things. The first time I met him I never would have guessed ... '

Tom did not finish the sentence. He was thinking of his father, and how little one knows what lies behind a face.

When the two boys reached the cabin, Muiris met them at

the door. '*Fáilte isteach,* Tomás. The children were afraid you had abandoned us.'

'I would never do that.'

Muiris put one hand on his shoulder. 'I know, lad. Bríd, see who has returned!'

In the blink of an eye Tom was surrounded by family. Bríd was offering food to him, Maura was tugging at his hand to get him to listen to her. Muiris was smiling at him.

For the first time since they met, Tom felt shy in his uncle's presence. While walking to the cliffs he had rehearsed what he would say. Memorised every word. Been confident of his reception because he knew Muiris.

Or did he? Who was behind that smiling face? Savages and barbarians, his father had said.

Tom dared not wait any longer for fear he would lose his nerve. *Plunge in.*

'You gave me my share of the spices,' he said to Muiris.

His uncle raised an eyebrow. 'I did, of course. Do you want more? I am afraid they are all gone now.'

'You never gave me a share of the gold.'

Tom was afraid Muiris might be angry, but he kept smiling. 'As much as any of us, Tomás, you are entitled to a share. But we only exchange a little of the gold at a time. We do not want to draw attention to ourselves.'

'I need money right now,' Tom insisted. 'Not for myself; for my mother. So she can keep her house.'

'I think we had best sit down,' said Bríd. She motioned to the stools beside the hearth.

With the exception of Maura – who busied herself trying to plait ribbons into her mother's hair – they all listened intently as Tom told of his father's misfortune. When he got to the part about the moneylender Muiris stopped him. 'Was that one of *Richard Boyle's* moneylenders?'

'Yes.'

Muiris slapped his thigh and roared with laughter. 'There's irony for you!'

Maura peered over her mother's shoulder. 'What's a sironey?'

'Irony,' her father said, still chuckling. 'Something with an unexpected twist. Tomás's father does not have enough money to repay Richard Boyle's moneylender, yet we have a fortune in gold we took from the self-same–'

Bríd frowned at him. 'Wee Maura does not need to know these details, Muiris.'

'The moneylender is not going to take our property anyway,' Tom tried to explain. 'Mr Fox is. He bought the mortgage on our house and land.'

Muiris stopped laughing. 'Mr Fox? Mr *Herbert* Fox?'

'The same. Why? Do you know him?'

'I know *of* him.' Once again Tom heard the sinister edge in his uncle's voice.

'Mr Fox and my father were in business together,' Tom said.

Muiris sat so still he might have been carved from stone.

Tom continued with the story as he knew it, including Elizabeth's engagement and William Flynn's confession. Even Maura was listening now.

Muiris never took his eyes from his nephew's face.

As Tom spoke, the pattern in the boy's mind was expanding. Filling in details. 'Mr Fox has wanted our land for a long time. It would give him a place where he can keep a closer eye on his business. I think his business is trading in stolen goods. He uses men and boats from his shipyard in Cobh to collect the loot smugglers store around the bay. Until my father went off to war, he was selling that merchandise in Dublin for Mr Fox.'

Muiris leaned forward. 'I swear to you, Tomás,' he said earnestly, 'I was unaware that your father was Fox's agent. We were but one of the links in a chain. Our only connection with Fox was through his boatmen. When we had valuable items for their market we left word at–'

'The Castle of Gold,' Tom interrupted.

His uncle's mouth dropped open. 'How could you know that?'

'The night you told me the story of the castle, you said we would not land there "this time". That could only mean you landed there at other times. What better place to leave secret messages than an abandoned castle people thought was haunted?'

'Muiris always said you have a head on your shoulders, Tomás,' Bríd remarked.

'I have a head too!' Maura piped up. She patted her unruly curls with both hands.

Muiris stroked his lower lip. 'You put me in an awkward position, Tomás. We have just brought the first money from Limerick. It is in this house tonight, waiting to be distributed to the members of our sept. It might be a year or two before we have the entire amount. Although I do not know how large the mortgage is on Roaringwater House, I can make a guess. You may need it right now, but your share of the money we have here might not be enough.'

Tom felt his heart sink. 'Are you certain?'

'Wait a moment.' Muiris went into the bedroom. There was a sound of furniture scraping across the packed earth floor.

Muiris returned. The timber box he carried was not much bigger than Catherine Flynn's tea chest. This one was not brass bound and highly polished. It was weathered and tied with a rope. Muiris set it on the table and untied the rope.

When he lifted the lid they saw that the chest was full of coins. Maura clapped her hands.

Muiris began removing the coins. 'This is a gold unite,' he said, holding up a gleaming coin. 'A new English coin, the equivalent of a sovereign. And these are old gold sovereigns. Here we have silver crowns and half crowns. And some shillings, because they are easier to spend. We do not accept anything smaller.'

While they watched, he arranged the coins into equal stacks on the dresser. 'This is my family's portion. This one belongs to Séamus and his wife, this is for Seán, this will go to Fergal and his parents, and this ...'

There was a stack of coins for every family in the narrow valley, as well as the six or seven others who lived farther up the river. The stacks were equal in size. When the chest was empty, Tom said, 'What about my share?'

'I planned to take it from my portion when we had all the money,' Muiris told him.

Tom's face fell. 'I can't wait until then. We'll be living ... I don't know where we'll be living in a year or two. But no place as nice as this.'

Donal shifted weight on his stool. Thought about the familiar cabin. The cosy sleeping loft, the shining delft on the dresser, the hen nesting contentedly in her box. Thought of Roaringwater House and the possessions he had envied. Made a decision. 'Is some of that money mine too?' he asked his father.

'It is, of course, and Maura's as well.'

Donal stood up. Stood tall. 'I already have everything I need,' he stated. 'Give my money to Tomás so he can keep his home.'

'Give Tomflynn mine too!' cried little Maura.

• • • • • • • • • • •

CHAPTER TWENTY-NINE

THE BATTLE IS JOINED

They beached the currach on the shingle below the cave.

'Thank you for helping me with the mortgage, Muiris,' said Tom.

His uncle replied, 'I have had no experience with them myself, but I do know a bit about sharp practice. Are you certain you want to handle things this way?'

'I am certain. I've been thinking about it ever since Mr Fox arrived.'

'Remember, Tomás, we know two important things about that man. He is a bully and he is greedy. Bullies are always cowards at heart. And greedy men always want more.'

Tom grinned. 'I'll remember.'

'I will be waiting at the top of the cliff. If I see a candle in your window I will know all is well, and I can go home. If I do not see a candle by the time the moon rises, I will come to you and sort things out myself. In my own way.'

There was a sinister edge to his voice. Tom found it comforting. 'I'll be all right,' he assured his uncle.

'One more thing, Tomás. When your mother married Liam Ó Floinn she became part of his family. Under our ancient laws she is no longer entitled to share the property of our sept. I broke the English law by smuggling. Now I choose to break Irish law,' Muiris said with a wry smile. 'As I divide the treasure I will put aside a full portion for Caitríona. It will be buried at the very back of this cave. Should she – or her children, Tomás – ever be in need, you will know what to do. 'Now go and drive the fox from his den.'

* * *

Tom entered the front door of Roaringwater House carrying a large leather bag. He found his family in the great hall. Herbert Fox was holding court in front of the fireplace, boasting of the way he had built his shipping business out of nothing. Sagging on her chair, Catherine Flynn sat twisting her hands. Her daughters huddled around her. William Flynn stood at the far end of the room, leaning against the wall. His face was ashen and his eyes were bloodshot.

They looked up when Tom entered. Without even glancing at Fox, the boy walked across the floor and handed the leather bag to his father. 'Here is what you wanted, sir,' he said.

Flynn stared blankly at him.

Tom raised his voice. 'Did you not ask me to fetch this for you?'

'Eh?' Flynn hefted the bag. Felt its weight. Heard the clink of metal.

Turning so Fox could not see his face, Tom winked at his father.

William Flynn opened the bag and peered into it. After a sharp intake of breath, he looked back at his son.

Tom silently mouthed a name. Ó Driscoll.

Flynn thought very fast indeed. When he spoke he kept his voice calm. 'Thank you, Tom,' he said, as if his son routinely handed him bags full of gold coins. Striding over to the Jacobean chest, Flynn poured out the coins in a gleaming cascade.

Herbert Fox's jaw dropped. 'Where did you get all that money?'

'I have resources,' Flynn replied without looking up. He was busily counting the coins atop the chest.

'You had better tell me the truth, Flynn. I can make things bloody hot for you,' Fox snarled.

Bullies are always cowards at heart. Tom cleared his throat. 'I come from an ancient and honourable family, Mr Fox. Kings in this land since before the before.'

His mother sat up straight in her chair.

Adding a sinister edge to his voice, Tom went on. 'Show my father respect or you will answer to relatives of ours whom you have never met before. They are quite close at hand. And they will not treat you gently.'

Herbert Fox cried, 'I will not be threatened by a mere boy!' He did not sound so sure of himself, however. He gazed uncertainly around the room, trying to decide what to do next. He started towards Mrs Flynn, but she drew back from him. The three girls swept their skirts aside as if he were dirty. He turned back to Flynn. 'What's this about the rest of your family? You never mentioned them before.'

Tom saw his father finish counting. Saw the naked greed on the face of Herbert Fox. *Greedy men always want more.*

'If you hope to collect any interest at all on your mortgage, Mr Fox,' Tom said, 'you will accept what my father is about to offer.'

'The total amount due,' Flynn announced, 'plus ten shillings.'

'Only ten shillings interest? That is robbery!'

'I would not accuse other people of a crime if I were you,' said Tom.

'I demand—'

'You are in no position to demand anything, Herbert,' Flynn interrupted. 'You heard my son. Give us any more trouble and I shall summon dangerous men you really do not want to meet.' He swept the money into the leather bag and handed it to Fox. When the man clutched the neck of the bag his knuckles were white.

Out of the side of his mouth Flynn asked Tom, '*Are* there any dangerous men nearby?'

'Absolutely,' the boy assured him.

Mr Flynn called out, 'Our guest must leave immediately, Simon! Send for his horse and escort him off my property. Sign this deed of acceptance, Mr Fox. That will be the end of our business forever.'

When he was certain that Fox had gone, Tom ran upstairs. He lit a candle and placed it in the window of his bed-chamber. Then he joined his family downstairs for a celebratory supper. Roast mutton and boiled onions and steaming hot plum pudding.

His parents made no effort to conceal their relief. His sisters were almost giddy with it. They asked Tom countless questions. At first he tried to put them off with vague answers, but his mother would not allow it. 'Secrets in a family can cause too much harm,' she said. 'Surely we have learned that much. Tell us the truth, Tom. Tell us all of the truth.'

So he did. Beginning with the day he ran away and fell down the cliff. He only paused to take bites of food – he found himself very hungry. When Tom told about joining the smugglers his father sputtered with anger. Mrs Flynn put her hand over her husband's. 'Tom did no worse than you have done, William,' she said.

'I was only trying to provide for my wife and children.'

'And your son was only trying to spread his wings,' she replied. 'That is perfectly natural. Go on, Tom. What happened next?'

By the time he finished relating his adventures the hour was very late. Tom was hoarse from so much talking. Caroline could not stifle a yawn. The table was covered with crumbs and only a smear remained of the pudding.

Mrs Flynn suggested they all go to bed.

Mr Flynn followed his son up the stairs. 'I have one more question to ask you, b ... Tom.'

The boy stopped and turned around. 'Yes, sir?'

'Obviously you approached your mother's people on your own and did some clever negotiating. I have to say, I am impressed, Tom. And sorry that I underestimated you. Very sorry.' Apology did not come easily to William Flynn. 'You could have brought the money to Fox yourself and claimed all the credit,' he went on. 'Many men would have done just that. Why did you deliver it to me instead?'

The boy was standing one step above his father, which put their faces on a level. He looked for a long moment into William Flynn's eyes. Recalled the broken man. Pitied him. And chose to love him.

Tom smiled. 'Because you are the man of the family, sir,' he said.

...harlanna Poibli Chathair Baile Átha Cliath

Dublin City Public Libraries

Leabharlanna Poiblí Chathair Baile Átha Cliath

Dublin City Public Libraries

HISTORICAL NOTES

Tom and Donal and their families are fictional, but Richard Boyle and his sons, Thomas Wentworth and King Charles were real people. In November 1640 Thomas Wentworth was impeached by the English Parliament. Accused of high treason, he was beheaded in May 1641.

In 1642 King Charles declared war on the English Parliament, and the English Civil War began. In 1649 King Charles was charged with high treason and beheaded by the victorious Parliamentarians under Oliver Cromwell. Richard Boyle, Earl of Cork, died in 1643. He was never reconciled with his son, Robert.

Sir Fineen Ó Driscoll, his story, and that of the Castle of Gold were real. Smugglers and pirates operated on Roaringwater Bay for many years. Some of the caves they used can still be found around the shores of the bay.

Sir Walter Raleigh was also real, and was a favourite of Queen Elizabeth. He lived for a while in Youghal, County Cork. A privateer and adventurer, he introduced both potatoes and tobacco into England from the New World. His recipe for 'Sack Posset' is quoted in a book called *Consuming Passions; A History of English Food and Appetites*, by Philippa Pullar.

Roaringwater House is modelled on several Munster country houses of the period. Bed-closets like Tom's were a popular way to keep warm at night. Children of his class were always dressed as miniature adults.

The cabin in which Donal and his family lived is based on cabins that were common in Ireland in the seventeenth century, and right up until the last century.

OTHER HISTORICAL NOVELS
from O'Brien Press

OTHER HISTORICAL NOVELS BY MORGAN LLYWELYN

This is the amazing story of Brian Boru, High King of Ireland. As a boy, Brian and his clan suffered terribly at the hands of the Danes, and he has sworn to rid Ireland of these invaders. At the battle of Clontarf he takes his revenge – but loses his life.

Bisto Merit Award – Historical Fiction

OTHER HISTORICAL NOVELS BY MORGAN LLYWELYN

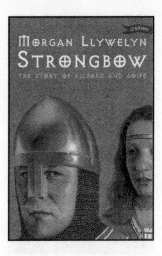

The story of the greatest Norman of them all – Strongbow. He was one of the first to come to Ireland. He captured Dublin and married an Irish princess – Aoife MacMurrough, the daughter of the King of Leinster. Alternate chapters are told from his and her point of view, thus illuminating both sides.

Reading Association of Ireland Award
Bisto Merit Award (Historical Fiction)

OTHER HISTORICAL NOVELS
BY MORGAN LLYWELYN

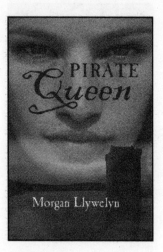

The story of the famous pirate, trader and clan leader Grace O'Malley – Granuaile – of west Mayo. With her fleet of ships, she patrolled the western coast and seas and held enormous power there. Most famously, she went to London to visit her main enemy, Queen Elizabeth, a meeting of the two most powerful women of the sixteenth century.

OTHER HISTORICAL NOVELS
BY MORGAN LLYWELYN

John Joe and Roger are pupils at Patrick Pearse's
famous school, St Enda's. It is 1916, and plans are
afoot for a rising against British power in Ireland.
Easter Week gives the boys their chance to fight
for Ireland, but they are forbidden to take part as
they are too young. Still, they get caught up in
the action anyway and see the dramatic events
first hand.

a contemporary novel
by MORGAN LLYWELYN

Suzanne and Ger come from different back-
grounds but they share a love of horses and a
burning ambition to succeeed in the tough
worlds of dressage and showjumping. Can
friendship too be part of that world?

OTHER HISTORICAL NOVELS FROM THE O'BRIEN PRESS

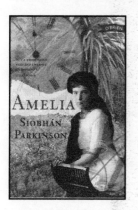

Almost thirteen, Amelia Pim is the daughter of a wealthy Quaker family. Her mind is filled with her forthcoming birthday party. But when her happy, privileged world is shattered, Amelia must learn to live with poverty – and even disgrace when her mother is arrested for Suffragette activity. But she also learns the value of true friendship.

It is 1916 and war has broken out both at home and abroad. Amelia, now sixteen, has to deal with the departure of her first love, Frederick, who has decided to fight in the First World War. Then servant girl Mary Anne's brother is hiding in their garden after his involvement in the Easter Rising ...

The story of the Flight of the Earls. It is 1603 and Hugh O'Neill is about to leave his homeland after the disastrous defeat at Kinsale. He wants his youngest son, Con, to go with him. But where is he?

Dublin 1922. Working class Annie Reilly is thrilled to win a scholarship to Eccles Street School. She meets Peter Scanlon, a student at Belvedere College. He sides with the rebels in the civil war, but when Annie's life is threatened, he has to decide where his loyalties lie.

Liam and Nora become friends at a feis ceoil. But their fathers are on opposite sides in the Dublin Lockout of 1913: one a striking worker, the other a wealthy employer. Can their friendship survive?

The ghost of fifteen-year-old Samuel Scott moves restlessly aboard the *Titanic* as she sails to her doom in 1912. An eye-witness to the final days in the lives of rich and poor, crew and passengers, this is Samuel's story.

When her father returns from the First World War he is shell-shocked. And now another war is being fought in her homeland – the Irish Civil War. Her father wants peace, but others want to fight to the bitter end. Who is right?

Kate is captivated by Irish dancing. It's the most exciting thing she's ever done – but in 1930s Ireland, not many people have the money for such luxuries. How can Kate follow her dream of dance?

In thirteenth-century Ireland, full of war and danger, four children are determined to stop Richard de Clare, Lord of Bunratty, killing the magical Silver Stag. Adventure, conflict and danger await them in their desperate struggle.

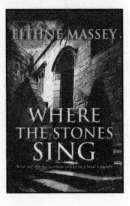

A vivid story of a fight for survival in darkest medieval Dublin. As the spectre of the Black Death hovers over the city, Kai is plucked from the filthy streets to sing in the great Christ Church choir. But Kai has a dark secret and there are dangerous enemies everywhere.

www.obrien.ie